A.N. PAYTON

Bubbles and Troubles

Contents

Chapter 1

My shoe slipped as I launched sideways, barely avoiding the lunge of the weapon aiming at my face. My knees cracked into the hard ground as I fell. I grimaced and an unwelcome huff slipped through my lips.

The sharp, salty scent of sweat mixed with the dirt as another strike streamed toward me. I dropped to my stomach, my sword flinging from my hand and landing several paces away. A woosh of air touched the back of my neck as my opponent's sword blew over the space my head recently vacated.

I pushed to my elbows and frantically tried to crawl toward my weapon.

The tip of a wooden training sword touched the side of my neck.

"Dead," Tyfin said.

The fight left me. I let my limbs fall to the ground, only slightly hoping it might open wide and swallow my aching body whole.

"You've gotta be faster than that, Rae." Krissa lounged in a short chair at the edge of the training circle. She'd wound her auburn hair into a thick braid across the top of her head, intertwined with fraying, colorful ribbons. Bubbles the warplog sat sideways on her lap, his long back legs draping off hers on the other side. He didn't stir at her words, too deep asleep.

I pushed to my knees. Rocks undug from my skin, replaced by bright red specks of blood. They matched the plethora of scabs already there perfectly.

"I am not *trying* to be slow," I said, the protest falling on deaf ears. Tyfin grabbed my training sword and offered a hand to help me up. I grabbed his palm despite the slight sting from my raw skin.

Krissa lifted a mug of an iced tea—which I'd prepared for her before practice—and let a shimmer of laughter light her eyes.

"You're doing good." Tyfin smacked his hand on my shoulder. I tried to hide the wobble through my tired knees. "You've only just started training. It can take years to become proficient with the blade, and a lifetime to master it."

He walked toward the water pitcher resting to the side. Krissa caught my gaze again and raised her brows, mouthing the words *a lifetime*.

I rolled my neck from side to side. The tight pull of the muscles felt good after so much work. A lifetime could be long, and I already live on borrowed time since escaping the capital—Erline—and its corrupt king over five years ago. If his Providers found me in Hallow's Promise, they'd drag me back to the capital, and I'd fare a fate worse than death.

Tyfin handed me a glass of water. Sunlight lit his hair and reflected from his smooth skin. I raised a tentative hand to my hair, which caught in my fingers. He looked calm and collected, and I looked like Brew ran me over.

"You'll be wielding that sword before you know it—without being a danger to yourself."

I gave him a smile, but it felt fake. My real silver sword rested inside Brew-Tea-Ful, my magic potion wagon, waiting for me to learn some basic techniques before I could carry it. I tried not to think about the mercenary who gave me the blade, his shining eyes, or how he smelled like fresh rain and forest.

"I'll see you next week?" Tyfin asked.

"I'll be here."

"Me too!" Krissa cradled Bubbles softly in her arms, avoiding waking the creature.

Tyfin disappeared into the armory adjacent to the training field, and we turned onto the cobblestone road of Oath Street. Brew waited just beyond the main road, nestled in the quiet neighborhood where a ley line ran.

"You know, I do think you're getting better," Krissa said.

"What gave you that impression? The first time I ate dirt, or the second, or the third?"

She smirked. "But there wasn't a fourth time, was there?"

I sighed. In some ways, she was right. I usually ended up on the ground more times than that during training. But I also wanted to see *real* progress, to complete a drill without smacking myself with the business end of a wooden sword.

Brew appeared through the trees. The wagon shuttered a bit at our approach, its way of saying hello. The rear door swung open of its own accord, though I'd been sure to lock it before leaving. Maybe Brew sensed my exhaustion and offered the best help it could.

"Are you going to the college?" Krissa hesitated at the doorway while I washed my hands in the basin.

The Central College for Mages and Magics was all that really put Hallow's Promise on any map. The sprawling campus offered a coveted education in the magical arts. It consumed almost a quarter of the town, and the students really enjoyed purchasing the drinks and potions I made.

"Yes. I want to get there before the noon bells. Do you want to ride with us?"

Krissa pressed her lips together, and the slightest green hue colored her face. She wasn't fond of Brew's method of travel. "No thanks, I'd rather walk. I'll meet you for dinner after my class."

Krissa taught statistics at the college. She looked too young to be a professor at a prestigious school and taught a class few wanted to take.

"Sounds good."

Krissa passed Bubbles to me and headed down the road. I watched her step back onto Oath Street before I closed the door. The floorboards cracked beneath my feet as Brew complained.

I patted the countertop. "She doesn't have to come with us if she doesn't want to. We'll see her later."

The wagon settled, temporarily pacified.

When Bubbles decided he wanted to stick around permanently, I removed the door from one of the Brew's lower cupboards and stuffed in a plush blanket I'd purchased from the market just for Bubbles. I knelt. He roused slightly, enough to hop from my arms and jump in a couple circles before settling onto the fabric with his rounded face peeking out. He looked at me, his tongue flicking up to lick one of his eyeballs.

"I love you too." I patted his head, which he nuzzled into my palm before promptly going back to sleep.

* * *

I usually set Brew in the central courtyard where the college established a flourishing koi pond—everyone passed through it to get to their classes. But when the days felt particularly hot, I had Brew go to the south side of the campus, where pockets of shade cooled the wagon.

A chorus of bells sounded from the tower of the college as I finished putting out the sign with the menu of today's available drinks. The spiraling bell tower rose taller than any other building in the city, and every day, it played a beautiful array of music at noon and midnight. Despite several protests from Hallow's Promise citizens, the dean refused to cancel the midnight bells. He claimed something about tradition, but most thought he enjoyed reminding Hallow's Promise how central the college was to the town.

Students shuffled from their classrooms in a half daze, staring at nothing in particular. Some of them saw Brew and abruptly changed directions like starved wolves heading toward a fresh kill. I almost saw the drool on their chins as they charged closer, armed with creased textbooks and the prospect of promised dreams.

One young man slugged forward with an armful of parchment and paused outside my raised sash. He looked into the wagon without seeing me and spoke with a flat voice.

"Will the anti-inSIPity really motivate me to pass midterms?"

I smiled, even as the vacant gaze continued. "It's charmed with a gentle encouragement spell, so even though it may not last until midterms, it may be enough to let you find your own motivation again."

He blinked, finally focusing. His lips curved into a lazy smile. "Yes, please, I'll take one."

"Great, just a moment."

Brew flipped open a couple of drawers as I dug the mortar and pestle from a cupboard. Rounded, thin fabric filters rested in one drawer, and I plucked a couple from the stack. I had a feeling the young man wouldn't be the only student requesting this drink.

I pulled out rosemary, a fresh lemon, and a basic peppermint tea stock. Once I removed the required ingredients, Brew snapped each drawer shut. I poured a healthy amount of the pre-made tea into a pot and set it over the fire to warm.

A herby scent of rosemary flooded the wagon as I tapped some into the bottom of the mortar. The herb protested a bit while I ground it, fighting back with its long, stalky strands, until I finished smashing it into a fine powder. I cut the lemon into slices.

The edges of the filter split apart, revealing an opening where I piled the ground rosemary and lemon inside. I set it over the top of a large mug.

Brew slammed a cupboard shut beside my head.

"Ouch." I covered my ears and shot the wagon a glare. "That was loud." I looked over my ingredients, wondering which one upset Brew.

"Not enough rosemary?"

I caught the cupboard before it could slam again.

"More lemon?"

The wagon vibrated, a slight purr only I heard.

"Fine, fine, more lemon." I tossed a second lemon slice into the filter, shuffled the peppermint tea from the flames, and slowly and carefully poured it over the fabric. The slow pour allowed the flavors to mix without compromising the delicate tea flavor with too much rosemary. A citrus edge of lemons blended all the flavors into a subtle delight.

I put the soggy filter to the side and closed my eyes over the glass. A sliver of my magic lifted and wrapped around the drink. It hesitated, waiting for me, and I pushed it ever-so-slightly into the beverage. It shimmered the color of molten gold for a moment.

The magic settled. A spot on my wrist suddenly itched, a phantom remnant of the potential my power really held. If I removed the concealment spell over my skin, the outline of a dagger would mark me, claiming me as one of the king's Providers—his own personal servant.

I'd escaped that life, but he still had a hold over me. If I used more than my common witch magic, the king could locate me immediately. He'd punish me severely, then use my magic to do horrible things.

I hid in Hallow's Promise to avoid him—at all costs.

The warmth of the tea seeped into my hands and soothed my mind as I lifted it to the customer.

"Five coins, please."

He peeled the coins from his belt and turned away before they clinked into the lock box. I watched the back of his head, hoping the drink helped realign whatever future he wished for.

"Next—"

A terrible scream erupted.

The short line gathered around Brew paused their mindless shifting. Some kind of life returned to the students' eyes as they strained their necks, searching for the cause of the scream.

They didn't have to wait long.

Krissa streaked from one of the college buildings, a coiled braid escaping her hair and whipping across her back. She paused when she reached the lawn, glancing around frantically. She locked onto Brew and headed straight toward me.

I gripped the edge of the counter. Whatever scared my friend had to be bad.

"Excuse me. Excuse me. Move it. MOVE! CAN'T YOU SEE I'M TRYING TO GET UP THERE!" Krissa's voice became more panicked as she pushed through the throng of unhappy people in line. She finally appeared at the sash, redness tinting her cheeks even as pale skin peeked beneath.

"A bidie." She gasped for air, turning every other syllable incoherent. "In da leectur haaal."

"I'm not sure—"

She leaned inside the wagon, stretched to the tips of her toes, and grabbed my forearm. I put my other hand over hers, her urgency mixing with my confusion.

"A *body*! In the lecture hall!" Though stressed, her second attempt was a lot clearer. "I figured the Crime Investigation *Expert* would want to know that!"

Who? I did a long blink.

Oh yeah, *me*.

Chapter 2

There was a body in the lecture hall.

The dead woman sprawled supine behind a wooden podium. Her upper body hid behind the item, leaving her feet exposed to the room. Her dim gray eyes looked up at the arched ceiling. She couldn't see the exposed beams lined with wooden planks to amplify the speaker's voice naturally. Nor did she smell the scent of spilled ink permanently infused into the carpet.

Leof scribbled something on a notepad and cursed when the tip of the quill poked a hole through the parchment.

Constable Castor sent a glare over his shoulder from the seats where he quietly spoke to Krissa. I got caught in his gaze, and he lifted one side of his lip in a scowl, but didn't say anything. His protests over my new position with Hallow's Promise's Sheriff's Station yielded no results. He'd settled on hating me silently, one glare at a time.

He turned back to Krissa, probably asking another question about her discovery of Magnolia's body.

"You knew her?" I asked.

Leof sighed. "Professionally. She taught Historical Magic on campus, but she has a lot of miscellaneous knowledge too. I've asked for her help with some cases in the past."

Multiple constables roamed the lecture hall. Several dealt with administrators and campus guards. The dean hadn't arrived yet.

"Magnolia Feron Galrod." Leof stepped beside me. "Age 68, taught for over 30 years. She was planning to announce her retirement next year."

"Has anyone identified her next of kin?"

Long ago, the capital erased individual responsibility for naming children. Parents continued to choose the first name, but all second names bore the surname of the mother, and last names from the father. They claimed it helped maintain orderly counting for the annual census, but I knew the king used them to track familial lineages of rebels—should their descendants consider another uprising.

"Not yet, but Castor's working on that next," Leof said.

I knelt beside the body. Magnolia's head leaned back slightly, exposing a gaping mouth. No blood or apparent wounds, though the mortician—Alivia—would perform a complete examination at the morgue. Magnolia's silken robe remained flat over her body, concealing any trace of lividity that may have stained the skin. Her ashen tone looked cold, unnatural. The scent had already started to turn, not putrid yet, but a sickly smell of fresh rot.

"She's been here for over half a day, but not longer," I said. "Decay has begun, but there's no skin slippage or evidence of insect activity. I'd expect both after a day or so. We'll have to see if there's anything beneath her body, but nothing else stands out."

I leaned closer, making uncomfortable eye contact with the dead woman. Her fingers curled with rigor mortis, locking all the muscles in her body stick straight. She looked limp and soft, but I knew touching her would be akin to stroking the cobblestoned roads outside.

"Magnolia," I said, breathing her name to her, one last time.

A flicker of familiarity rebounded at the sound. Names held power—one of the many reasons I rarely used the capital's name—and some lingering trace of magic fluttered.

I sat back on my heels.

"Magic?" Leof asked.

"Can you sense it?"

He nodded. "Slightly. I didn't want to say anything to sway your observations though."

I pressed my lips together, but didn't reply. Leof had tested me several times since I'd accepted his offer of working at the Sheriff's Station with him, and I grew less pleased each time.

"Can you make a magic cast?" he asked, oblivious to my annoyance.

Every magic user created their own impression of power when they used their talents. I'd trained to recognize those marks—almost a fingerprint made of magic—and cast them into a physical form. If the marshal found a suspect, we could create a cast of their power and determine if the two matched. However, the art of comparisons was delicate and coveted, and I'd never had a desire to specialize.

"I can make the cast, but I'm not an expert at comparison. You'll need someone specially trained to infer any leads from it and make the final identification once we get a suspect. Do you have an expert?"

Leof looked down at Magnolia's body and gestured toward her.

"Damn," I said.

"Don't worry about the comparison," he said, scribbling on

his parchment again. "I'll find a new expert to look at it later. Just make the magic cast now so we can give the body to Alivia. She's already sent messengers asking when she can expect it."

A shiver went down my spine. The mortician and I reached an understanding long ago, but she still made me itch sometimes.

"I'll do the magic cast, and—"

"What is the meaning of all this?" A loud male voice boomed from the rear of the lecture hall at the top of a short set of stairs. Perthum, Dean of the Central Campus of Mages and Magics, strode inside with more confidence than any constable on the scene. His deep violet robes swished around his legs, releasing a musty scent of wet socks and stale water. "This is a prestigious educational institution, not a lounge for rubberneckers!"

Leof stepped toward the stairs. "Dean Perthum—"

Perthum turned his heated gaze on the werewolf. Leof shut his mouth, possibly a first.

"Don't you *Dean Perthum* me, Marshal Leof." He strung out the title, turning it into a subtle mock. "I remember when your little paws first stepped foot on this campus. Just because they're larger now doesn't mean you have any more power here than back then."

Leof shrunk away. He twisted the quill and parchment, his mouth opening and closing, but nothing escaped.

Perthum puffed out his chest and let his voice boom through the room again. "Everyone that is not essential to this investigation at this moment must leave immediately! I refuse to see less than half of you exit the premises, or I will call our Security Spellcraft expert to make that happen!"

The constables and corporals looked at Leof. The wolf remained quiet before me, his head ducked. Others shuffled out in a line of quiet, confused whispers.

Castor helped Krissa stand. "I'll take her to the station and finish the interview there. She's probably seen enough here, anyway."

Leof took a step toward the door. I lunged to my feet and grabbed his shoulder.

"*You* are essential," I hissed.

The marshal stopped, pink coloring tinting his cheeks.

"Of course, I was just . . . moving."

Once enough investigators cleared the lecture hall, Dean Perthum faced us. His satin gaze showed clear disapproval at our presence, as though he alone should be in the room with the dead woman, by the mere responsibility of heading the college.

He finally looked at Magnolia. All the fight fled from his sharpened gaze, giving it a clouded, saddened look. He walked closer to her body, pausing at the bottom step, and put a hand over his mouth.

"Do you know what happened?" he asked softly.

"Magic," Leof said. My eyes widened. That was confidential information, not prepared to be shared with the public. "We're going to make a magic cast, but that's all the evidence we can collect from here."

"Magic," Perthum whispered.

"Sir," I said, since Leof apparently felt more like a student than a marshal at the moment. "Did Magnolia have any enemies, significant others, or financial plans after retirement?"

Perthum sank into one of the chairs along the edge of the staircase. The wood groaned beneath him, but he didn't flinch.

He offered a stiff laugh. "You must have heard about Magnolia's statement of retiring. She retracted it almost immediately. That woman never planned to retire, I'm sure. As far as enemies, yes, she had several, but no spouse. Academia is cutthroat, more than people want to admit, and Magnolia grew a thick skin. Everyone fights for the best journal to publish with, the best sheriff or mayor to employ their skill set."

"Is there anyone in particular she competed with? I'm sorry. I'm sure this is hard to talk about."

Perthum took another look at me. His eyes narrowed.

"I didn't catch your name," he said.

I smiled and held out my hand. "Rae, Crime Investigation Expert."

"Expert?" He raised a brow. "Are you replacing him?" Perthum stuck his thumb toward Leof.

The exchange appeared to revive the wolf. He shivered from head to toe, and when his gaze returned to the Dean, the marshal was back.

Finally.

"Perthum, I have a few more questions about your staff that require detailed answers."

"I'm not convinced you have that kind of authority."

"I assure you that I do. In fact . . ."

Leof and Perthum's conversation slipped out of my focus. Despite the few investigators left in the room, the low chatter of voices behind me, and the sudden intensity Perthum brought to the room, it faded into only me and Magnolia.

I crouched beside her again. I let my palm hover over her face, feeling the traces of foreign magic lingering along her skin. No remnants of pain or suffering. Disliked, cutthroat, or not, she had been someone's daughter, family, friend. Someone stole her life.

My magic unfolded. Death called me—it always had. Despite

attempting to run and hide from it, I recognized the potential now. I could help people, maybe not Magnolia, but anyone that did or ever cared for her.

I had a magic cast to make.

Chapter 3

While the dean and marshal talked, I walked back to Brew and collected the supplies for a basic casting kit. Magic casts weren't particularly difficult to make, but the preservation substance tended to be fragile, and disliked moisture of any kind. The creation would be simple enough—the preservation, another story.

I set out a box of freshly milled flour beside a large pitcher of water. The box of salt perched beside the pair.

I stepped back and examined Magnolia's body to make sure I'd found any other visible evidence. We couldn't move her until after the cast, but the process could taint lingering clues. Nothing jumped out at me, besides the bitter magic surrounding her body.

The metal ladle had sunk into the flour, and it took a few minutes to extract from the depths. White powder covered my hands, but I scooped the tool until it overflowed. With my free hand, I grabbed a sifter.

I started at Magnolia's face. Magic was viscous, but slow like glass. Over time, the lines may shift or wear away. They also tended to pool in certain places along the body—particularly the face.

Flecks of white dust settled across her features. The flour

sunk into her eyes and her exposed mouth, nestling along the age-lines of her neck. Magnolia didn't care. She remained still, stiff, unyielding to anything life offered.

Once I encased her entire body in flour, I turned to repeat the process with the salt.

"What is the meaning of this?" Dean Perthum leapt from his seat, and his face turned instantly red.

I hesitated, but Leof seemed content to stand quietly to the side again.

"I'm making a magic cast to document the impression left behind from whatever power killed her."

His bushy brows creased. "Will this desecrate the body? She deserves to be returned to her loved ones."

"The body will remain preserved," I vowed. "I can assure you that the powder is temporary."

"It had better be." The dean crossed his arms. The edges of his robes slipped up, a bit too snug around the shoulders. "Or the Sheriff's Station will hear the full complaints of this college."

I gave a hard smile and turned to the marshal. "Do you have a casting tray?"

"Eloso, get a tray," he barked and one of the constables I didn't know disappeared beyond the doorway.

The pressure weighed heavier as Perthum's gaze fell on me. I finished adding salt to the body and grabbed the pitcher.

"Surely, you do not—" Perthum started.

Leof finally interrupted. "Let my investigator work, Perthum."

The dean's mouth snapped shut, but his face stayed red.

I uncoiled my magic as I tossed the water into the air. Gasps rang through the lecture hall, echoing into a thousand audible splinters as they shattered against the elevated wooden beams. My power caught the liquid droplets—a choir of surprise welcoming their escape from gravity.

Simple elemental spells weren't enough for the king to find me—at least, he hadn't yet. I was careful not to push my limits, to only use casual magic, and never my secret abilities.

The water pushed and pulled against me as I flattened it into a long sheet over Magnolia's body. It hovered over her, waiting to connect with the flour and salt mixture that would eventually harden into a physical form.

Unfamiliar magic called to me as well—the remnants of whatever had killed the professor. I let my power entwine with it, carefully lifting the traces from her body and into the air. Flour and salt rose alongside the magic, levitating a few finger lengths above the body.

I slowly allowed the water sheet to lower. The flour and salt touched it where the magic lifted. They formed a thick paste. Intricately woven lines blended together, with parts and splits, and indentations, and reformation. The cast was beautiful, dainty, and lace-like, as intricate as any bride would wear on their Union Day. Magic didn't care if it crafted to kill or create. Like any tool, it existed for our use, and our humanity tainted it.

Eloso stepped up with a huge metal tray gripped in both hands. The longest edge of the tray stretched beyond his height, and the protruding sides were slightly wider than his body.

He set the metal on the ground beside the body. I lowered the cast onto it. Once all the thickened putty touched the metal, my magic pulled the excess water away. Only the design remained, the magic pattern ready to be compared to any suspects.

The water splashed to the ground beside the podium. I didn't train in elemental magic, and my precision wasn't good enough to funnel it back into the pitcher. Besides, it was worth seeing Perthum's smug face pinch as his lecture hall got a little wet.

"It'll need to dry until tomorrow night. Then it'll be firm enough to be examined. Don't—"

"Get it wet or bend the mold," Leof jumped in. "I know, I know. It's not my first magic cast."

I rolled my eyes. "Good, then you should know where to find an expert to compare the cast with any future suspects. Help me roll the body over so I can go find Krissa."

Leof and I hovered on each side of Magnolia's body. I carefully used a bit of magic to pile the lingering flour dust off her body and onto the floor. The werewolf grabbed her upper arm and turned her over.

Purple, red stains ran along her back where the blood pooled after death. Livor mortis, claiming the body had remained unmoved after death. No spilt blood beneath the body, either. Only magic struck her.

"Okay," I said, stepping back.

A flash of movement caught my eye as Leof released the body.

"Wait!" I caught her shoulder before she sank back to the ground. The unearthly coldness soaked into my hand, etched with death. My power licked it happily, recognized this magic, and wanted to draw it to myself.

She can come back, it whispered to me. *One life can buy another.*

I shook off the thoughts. They usually resided in a locked place at the rear of my mind, but occasionally, the temptation slipped through. I *could* bring Magnolia back—at the price of someone else's death.

I was no reaper to deal in life and death. I only investigated it.

The object moved again, a subtle slip of torchlight off a shiny surface. Caught at the waistband of her shirt sat a tuft of dark gray hairs.

"Get me a jar." I urged the hairs—or possibly fibers—from Magnolia's body. Eloso twisted the lid from a jar, and I plopped the evidence inside. I watched as he twisted the jar shut.

"What is it?" Leof claimed the glass and held it to the flickering light.

"I'm not sure. Would you mind scent mapping it?"

"You're asking me to find a magic cast comparer *and* do a scent map? You're the one with 'Expert' in the title."

I let out a sigh, but I didn't feel like arguing with Leof tonight. The infrequency of using my power in quantities beyond enchanted teas left me exhausted. Most witches built up their tolerance, a muscle that strengthened constantly. My magic muscle was rather weak and flaccid. I was tired.

"I'll take the cast back to my office and get Krissa. You can let me know when you finish your tasks."

The exterior door at the top of the stairs bounced open with a snap. We all turned toward it, the constables with their hands on their sword hilts. I pressed my lips together. Maybe one day I'd reach for my own weapon with such confidence instead of worrying about smacking myself with my own blade.

A constable walked in, with Bubbles frantically wiggling in his outstretched hands.

"Does anyone know what this is?" he asked, nose wrinkling. "I found it outside. It sort of smells."

Bubbles used his hefty back legs to smack the constable in the face. The man released him with a grunt, and the warplog landed on his back, unalarmed.

His beady little gaze fixed on the body behind me.

"Oh no, you don't!"

I ran up the stairs as the creature righted himself. His eyes grew big and glossy, and he opened his mouth. The lipless hole grew wider, wider than a creature his size deserved, exposing the rows of razor teeth. Bubbles would happily eat Magnolia, despite having had two rotten cow legs earlier in the week.

I dove at the warplog before he opened his maw completely. I pushed his top and bottom jaws together, then bopped the tip of his rounded nose lightly. The acid saliva didn't even drip onto my skin this time.

"No," I said, firmly. "We do not eat the victims."

"Or the suspects!" Leof called.

"Of course," I replied, but leaned closer to Bubble's head to whisper. "Don't listen to him. You can eat all the bad guys you want."

I scooped him up, and he twisted to find a comfortable spot. He looked longingly over my arm toward the body that two constables lifted into a dark linen bag.

"I'll get you some snacks from the butcher's shop tomorrow. How's that sound?"

Bubbles shifted his beady eyes to me and licked them, one at a time, without breaking eye contact.

"That sounds good to me too, Bub. Now let's go get Krissa."

I was afraid if I put Bubbles down, he'd go straight back to eat Magnolia's body, so Eloso carried the magic cast on its tray and set it on Brew's floor.

Once Brew's door latched, I gave Bubbles a good sniff. He didn't smell *that* bad.

Chapter 4

The Sheriff's Station sat on the east side of Hallow's Promise, at the end of Main Street, but not close enough that the fading paint and unwashed windows chased potential customers away from downtown. In wintertime, ice crystals perched along the slanted roof and adorned the building in rainbow swirls. But on a hot evening like tonight, the walls looked stifling and smelled like musty water.

A few constables greeted me in the hallway after I pushed the front doors open. I returned smiles at them while I passed the entryway desk, which remained empty, as always. Beyond the entrance, rows of doors spread from the center hallway. The second door belonged to Leof, who had a set of windows and a fireplace. I wished I could lounge in his plush chairs and study the fire while we contemplated wild theories about cases.

Instead, I knocked on the first door and waited for Castor to let me in.

"A moment," his deep voice filtered out, sending an immediate warm buzz of anger through me. He'd hated me since the first scene we worked together, and his dislike only grew after Leof hired me at the station.

I twisted the handle anyway. Locked.

I ground my teeth. His voice mixed with Krissa's softer tone, muffled with sounds of crying between words. I didn't trust the man with my friend, especially after she'd experienced such a deep trauma.

Cool metal of the lock brushed against my skin as I set my palm over it. I took a breath, and the fresh oxygen ignited the power deep in my soul. The delicate strings of magic unwound and sank into the lock at my gentle direction.

Pins snapped with an audible clink. The bolt unlatched.

I stepped inside and Castor stood from his chair. A red tint covered his face.

"She's done talking to you now." I kept my words hard and without room for an argument.

The constable stalked forward. His gaze fixated on me. Hatred twisted his brows at the center where a peppering of sweat shone.

"We're not done yet."

I crossed my arms. "I say you are."

"You don't have authority here."

A brush of my magic whipped around his skin. The man paused an arm's length from me and tensed. For whatever reason, he particularly hated magic.

"Tell me again how little authority I have." An edge of vibration lined the words, the threat.

Castor's face flattened. He took a smaller step and grabbed my upper arm lightly. He leaned down enough for his lips to brush my ear. My body locked tight, waiting to see what happened next.

"You're too close to this case," he whispered. The smell of soap and mint tinted his breath. "It's going to make you biased."

I leaned away and studied his hand on my arm.

"Let me go."

He hesitated for a moment. Then his fingers slipped off my arm, and the constable shouldered past me through the doorway.

I let out a sigh as he left. Krissa watched with a dark expression from a low wooden chair beside a long desk. She dabbed a handkerchief at her wet eyes.

"Come on." I gently took her hand in mine. "Let's talk in my office. You can hold Bubbles while I put some evidence away."

* * *

Leof's office lived at the heart of the building, central only to the Sheriff himself—who was usually at the capital promoting some political agenda, and not in Hallow's Promise at all. I had to cross two more hallways and go through the fitness room to reach my small office.

The hinges complained as Krissa encouraged the door open. Bubbles blinked his little eyes when she lit the single torch inside while I wrestled the magic cast into the tight space. I had a desk, but it was mostly empty, which made a great place to settle the metal sheet down.

I poked one of the edges of the fresh cast. The plaster started to dry, but it would take several more hours to fully cure.

An old purple couch consumed the other half of the room. I didn't have windows or a fireplace, so Krissa spread a quilted blanket over her lap and around Bubbles' feet. The warplog rested on her chest with his face nuzzled in her neck, as though sensing her turmoil.

I knelt beside her. "What happened?"

Silver tears welled in her eyes. "I was supposed to have the first lecture in the hall today, but the door was open when I got there. I called out. Nobody answered, so I assumed someone left it unlocked by accident. When I walked to the front, I . . . I saw her."

Krissa made a terrible noise through her nose, then wiped her eyes with the handkerchief. "I don't even know why I'm so upset."

"Someone you knew died. It's normal to be upset."

"Yes, of course, but I didn't even like Magnolia." She gave a little laugh, nothing humorous in the sound. "She was actually quite mean. When she announced her retirement, I put in an application for one of the boards she was on. After retracting her retirement, all she said to me was 'maybe someday,' then she laughed. Right in my face."

I creased my brows. "That's . . . really rude."

Krissa nodded. "I know! And when Professor Haggard congratulated her, Magnolia rolled her eyes and almost stepped on his toes when she walked off."

"So, she had a lot of enemies at work?"

"That might be an understatement. But since you're investigating, you should start with Professor Dominic Rune."

"Why?"

"Dominic and Magnolia had a relationship—if the woman was even capable of that. She called it off years ago, but he couldn't let her go. He basically stalked her, leaving little gifts that got more and more strange. Magnolia called them 'cute.'" Krissa shuttered. "More like creepy."

It sounded like Leof and I had a growing list of suspects to investigate. I made a mental note to check the door to the lecture hall for possible fingerprints, but it could wait until tomorrow. The constables would secure the scene for the night, and I needed to get Krissa somewhere she felt safe. I didn't have much experience being a good friend, but I tried to learn more every day.

"Was Castor respectful to you?"

"He was nice, actually." She stroked the top of Bubbles' back, where little knobby bones spread below the scaled skin. "He asked about Magnolia, my job, the students, basic stuff—all the same things you asked, actually. I barely felt like I was being interrogated."

An itch spread beneath my skin. Why had Castor said I'd be too close to the case? I pressed my lips.

"Do you want to stay with me tonight?" I asked.

Krissa looked at me and visible relief crossed her face.

"Doesn't Bubbles snore?"

"Yes," I answered, more honest than anything I'd said today. "He snores terribly loud, all night long."

She chuckled softly, carefully moving to avoid waking the sleeping warplog.

"Then I'd love to stay with you tonight."

Chapter 5

Sunlight streaked through the windows of my cottage at the first rays that slipped over the city wall. A golden hue illuminated my bottles and jars, sending melancholy herbs into a cascade of deep greens and browns with an occasional brighter yellow or blue.

I ran the sharp tip of a knife down a long vanilla pod. The brown bean split in half, releasing the raw sweetness of the flavor. Distilled booze I'd purchased from the market waited in portioned glass bottles. Once I'd sliced enough beans, I slipped them into the first bottle and snapped the cork on tight. The syrup needed to rest for a few months before use.

Krissa and Bubbles slept in the upstairs loft. All three of us had stuffed into my bed, which was not large enough for two adults and a warplog. After a few hours, I'd retreated to the couch on the main floor. The fire adjusted itself into a low flame, which warmed my body enough to finally relax and catch some sleep.

Now the flames licked the top of the cauldron I'd slipped into the simmering stand. Usually, the pots contained syrups, flavorings, or small potions to sell with Brew. This batch held a healthy portion of homemade oatmeal. I'd harvested my own crop earlier in the season and stored the grains for the perfect morning, which felt like today.

I took one of the vanilla pods and tossed it straight into the thickening oats. It bubbled with the rich flavor. I poured a good amount of molasses into a mortar and topped it with sugar I'd extracted from cane last week. Crushing the ingredients against the unyielding stone felt familiar, relaxing. The white crystals absorbed the softened sap until they faded into a warm, amber brown.

A little pull on my wards warned me that someone had entered my property. After a killer broke into my house and ransacked everything, I'd studied more advanced wards and set an excess amount around the land. I'd bet not even Valen—the annoying mercenary at the root of all the feelings I tried not to think about—could surprise me again.

Three taps sounded against the door. I finished grinding the sugar. I refused to feel rushed to greet my uninvited visitor. If they even attempted to open the door against my will, they'd meet a very severe case of Lightning-Crotch. I smiled at the thought. I hope someone tried one day.

The bed squeaked as Krissa sat up. Bubbles complained about the interruption beside Krissa with a half squawk, half groan. I rinsed my hands in the basin and wiped them on a clean rag.

Fresh morning air promised another hot day when I opened the door. Leof stood there, a frown across his face, and his hands stuffed in the pockets of his breeches. His expression changed to an apologetic grimace.

Castor stood behind the marshal with his arms crossed.

I raised my brows and waited silently. A thick dread pooled at the bottom of my chest. An early morning visit from Castor promised to sour the rest of the day.

"Tell her," Castor said, tone too clipped to be talking to his superior.

But Leof didn't respond. He sighed instead.

"Is Krissa here?" he asked.

It was my turn to cross my arms. "Why?"

"We need to ask her a few more questions about last night."

I narrowed my eyes. The werewolf didn't look like an investigator readdressing a prime witness. His brows dipped in a sorry state, and he glanced everywhere except at me.

"Why?" I asked again, harder, firmer.

Castor pushed forward and ducked his face to mine. "She's officially being questioned as a suspect in Magnolia Feron Galrod's murder."

Heat seeped through my limbs and twisted a very dark part of me, right at the center of my soul. I could rip Castor's life from his body before the constable could blink. It would take moments. It would feel so, so good . . .

It would lead the king right to me.

"You know magic was the cause of her murder," I said. "Krissa couldn't have done that."

"There are plenty of magical criminals available for hire." Castor glanced over his shoulder where Brew sat beside the house. "It doesn't even require any real skill."

"Leof?" I asked. "You can't believe this."

The werewolf finally looked at me. "There are some questions, Rae. Krissa wanted a board position Magnolia held, and they were professional competitors. The sooner we can talk to her, the sooner we can prove she wasn't involved."

"You're not welcome in my home." I put power into the words. The wards bristled—the Lightning-Crotch eager for its first victim.

A soft hand touched my arm. Krissa pulled the door wider and stepped beside me. She jerked her chin up, the redness from her eyes faded.

"I have nothing to hide," she said. "I'll go with you."

I grabbed her fingers. "Don't—"

She squeezed my hand. "I'm fine, Rae. I'll be back soon."

Leof led Krissa down my stoop. The anger churned and twisted inside me, only my friend's words preventing me from making a terrible, dangerous decision.

Castor lingered. "I told you that you were too close," he said, then followed the others.

The marshal helped Krissa onto his horse, Cherry, while Castor climbed onto his mount. She gave me one more wave before the animals turned toward the road.

Then, the three were gone.

I shut the door slowly, carefully.

An image of Castor's grave flashed in my mind. Leof was doing his duty as the marshal, but I knew Castor made the accusations. He didn't have any evidence and lacked a true motive—beside his hatred for me.

I climbed back upstairs and changed into a simple black tunic and loose linen pants. I snuggled Bubbles for a moment, then set him on his little bed beside the couch. He looked at me with those beady eyes. He had an unspoken question in that look, but I couldn't take him with me to the college. The lingering evidence of Magnolia's body would make the warplog hungry, and I didn't have time to make it to the butcher shop tonight.

A thick scent made me pause.

The oatmeal glowed softly beneath the embers of the fire.

"Turn it off," I said. "I'm not hungry anymore."

As the flames died completely, I reached for the knob. I hissed, air escaping through tight teeth, and turned my arm to look for a wound.

The outline of a dagger flashed on my skin—my anger had seared away the concealment spell. The mark of a Provider blared for anyone to see.

I smiled. The mark used to represent entrapment, pain, and death. Today, it showed my determination and abilities to protect my friend.

But I couldn't let anyone else see it. Having the king and all his Providers descend on Hallow's Promise wouldn't help clear Krissa from any wrongdoing.

I drew deep breaths until my heart calmed and the rage eased from an inferno into a roaring flame. The concealment spell snapped into place, hiding evidence of my past and my secrets.

I opened the door and headed back to where Magnolia was murdered.

Chapter 6

An eerie silence spread over the usually bustling campus. They'd canceled classes for the day to hold a ceremony for Magnolia's passing. Tomorrow, students would hurry through the halls and worry about upcoming examines, but today was for Magnolia.

I spread a dark fabric across the stone floor before the doorway to the lecture hall. Krissa said the door was ajar when she arrived. The perpetrator may have left it open to conceal any noises while fleeing the scene of their crime. If they'd touched the wood, their fingerprints may remain on the substance.

I lit a stubby stick candle with a snap of my fingers and the barest pulse of magic. A thick scent of burning lard oozed from the wick. I wrapped a swatch of cotton fabric around my other hand, persuaded my bound fingers to grip the top of an old ceramic bowl, and allowed the flame of the candle to lick along the dish. Black soot spread up the side, the gamey lard scent turning to dense smoke.

My usual method of developing fingerprints was to conceal the item of interest in an enclosed space along with a dish of warming adhesive. As the adhesive paste heated, it vaporized into the air and caught along the oils and grease that composed the fingerprints. The process not only stabilized the prints but also allowed me to examine them more clearly for comparisons later. This door was far too large for that process. Even if I had a chamber large enough to contain the entire surface, the adhesive fumes may never collect enough to cover it all.

So, I had to make my own print powder.

Once enough dark ash stained the bowl, I exchanged the candle for a sharpened knife. The edge of the blade sent vibrations through my fingers as I carefully slid it along the dark streaks on the ceramic. Black powder flaked from the bowl and cascaded into a small dish settled below.

The process was long and painful. My fingers cramped with each new strike against the ceramic bowl. Hardly any ash cascaded into the collection dish. The slowness gave me time to pause and think.

I needed to find something that would quickly clear Krissa's name beyond any doubt. Despite the ridiculousness of the accusation, each moment spent investigating the wrong suspect took away an opportunity to find the right person. The rhythm of the knife against the bowl became a mantra inside my mind.

Find the evidence, find the evidence, find the evidence.

But what if I couldn't?

I muffled the dark, quiet voice in the depths of my head. It was the same one that spoke out all my fears should the king find me and slaughtered my friends one by one.

The last of the black streaks floated into the small pile of accumulated powder. I pushed aside the anger and dangerous thoughts and returned the bowl to hover above the candle. Heat seeped from the warm ceramic into the wad of cotton protecting my skin from the flames.

I repeated the process again and again until a decent amount of soot stacked into a pile on the collection dish. The painstaking amount of time allowed a calmness to smother the rage, at least a little.

A clear glass vile held a bit of fine, white powder. I'd made the cornstarch months earlier for a particularly tricky recipe, which I'd eventually given up trying to produce. I was glad for the failure now.

I heaved a hefty amount of cornstarch into a small spoon and added it to the soot pile. I blended them together until the mixture turned into a muted gray color. It would provide the perfect contrast to the painted door.

Footsteps echoed from farther down the hall as I dipped a long-bristled brush into the powder. I recognized the footsteps easily.

"I knew I'd find you here." Leof stopped beside me, smartly beyond the range the tiny blade may extend.

"Don't you have to interrogate someone you once called a friend?" My tone came out snappy, sharp.

Leof sighed. The marshal squatted beside me and ducked his head, defeated.

"Krissa *is* my friend. You know what an asshole Castor can be. The sooner he realizes she couldn't be involved, the sooner his motivation to find the real killer will come. He's stubborn as a mule, and about as attractive as one."

I snorted. A light coating of powder clung to the tips of the brush. Too much powder concealed the prints completely, rendering them useless.

"You didn't say that when you both showed up at my front door." I swished the brush between my fingers until they gained enough momentum to fan out wide.

"I'm still a marshal, Rae. I have to do my job."

I rose and stepped to the door. The long bristles flung into an arched circle as I spun the brush faster and let the very tips kiss along the wooden surface.

"Whatever helps you sleep at night, Marshal," I said, flatly.

Leof moved beside me again. He watched my hand, but I knew he studied every motion of my body.

"I'm here to help you. I knew Castor would bully her if they went alone, and I wanted to prevent that." Leof caught my wrist. I paused, the bristles falling from the door. "Let me help you, Rae. Let me in."

A memory I tried to repress roused at his words.

'Tell me something real, Valen.'

'I didn't come here for the Provider. I came here for —'

"Fine." The word sounded harsher than I expected, but the werewolf relaxed. His grip on my arm loosened, and I caught a glimpse of relief. "If you help me prove Krissa's innocence, I may reconsider ending our friendship. But if Castor ever knocks on my door again, he and his crotch are going to be sorry."

Leof's face flattened. "I don't know what that means."

"You better hope you never find out."

He released me, the lingering warmth still on my skin. I resumed my swirling and spread the powder higher up the door.

"Krissa's home already," Leof said into the silence. "Castor wanted to hold her until morning for more questions, but I stopped that immediately. She's not in custody, but we've asked her to remain in Hallow's Promise until the investigation is wrapped up."

A knot in my chest loosened. Krissa was home and safe, and

I would see her tomorrow. Then we would catch whoever threatened her freedom.

And killed Magnolia, of course.

He continued. "I've also sent a letter to a magic cast comparison expert. I should hear from her in the next few days. The cast may have some details about the type of magic that was used."

Gray powder covered the entirety of the door and formed a soft snow-kissed texture across the stone floor beneath my work. I sat back to look for any potential lines and shapes indicating a lingering fingerprint.

There was nothing on the door. Or rather, there were too many prints to siphon any individual ones out.

I sighed.

"I'm guessing that's not good?" Leof asked.

"No. There's nothing helpful here."

I pushed the brush into the powder dish too hard. It caught the lip and tipped the dish, spreading cornstarch and soot over my black fabric. Wonderful. Just *wonderful*.

Leof snatched a cloth before I grabbed it. Amber wolf eyes peeked from within his soul.

"What's wrong, Rae? I know Krissa being investigated is frustrating, but I think there's something more."

I pressed my lips together. Leof's job required him to read people like books, and he was good at it. So many things felt wrong, but thinking of Valen hurt more tonight than usual. The mercenary had broken into my house, threatened me, followed me—but also protected me, complimented me, gave me tools to learn to defend myself. And he was gone. I had never wanted to see him again, but the thought hurt.

"I had a life here, Leof. And now it's all changing."

"Change isn't bad, Rae. It's just different."

I snorted. "Give me my supplies. I'm heading home before restarting the investigation tomorrow. Brew-Tea-Ful is reserved for a party tomorrow night, so I need to prepare stock for that too."

Leof arched his brows but handed my things back. "You're going to cater a party in the middle of a murder investigation?"

"Sounds like a normal day to me." I stood, my legs complaining from sitting so long after all the swordsmanship training. "Tell Suzie I said hi."

"I won't. She hates you."

I laughed. Leof's daughter, Suzie, did hate me, and not completely unjustified. I'd gotten Leof into some trouble, and she blamed me. In her defense, so did I.

I didn't turn back as I left, my satchel of investigation supplies draped over my shoulder. I'd also stuffed the sword Valen had given me inside, not because I believed in my skills should I need it, but because sometimes, when I moved the leather hilt too close to my face and a bit too fast, I caught the faintest scent of evergreen.

Dusk had fallen. I'd been at the college all day, making fingerprint powder, applying it to search for evidence and found nothing. A waste, the whole day. Creeping shadows wandered along the perimeter of the campus and stretched toward the center. Brew waited on the far side of the courtyard. It had lit a candle for me, visible through the half ajar wooden sash.

Twigs snapped at my back. I paused and sighed. Leof must have followed me, probably with more questions or reassurances. Friendship was new to me, but it involved a lot more talking than I'd expected.

The snaps morphed into crunches over the dried leaves, then rhythmic steps at a faster speed. I turned, mouth open, but my tongue froze at the sight.

It wasn't Leof at my back, stalking me in the dark—it was something much worse.

Chapter 7

The creature dripped from the darkness, shadows personified and formed into a canine beast made of liquid ink. Bright green eyes pinned me with a predator's stare—as though it scented my blood and knew how rich it tasted.

I lifted my hands and crouched, keeping my body still. My heart thundered in my chest as a sharp jab of adrenaline turned my limbs light.

The beast tilted its head, like it heard the increase of the rhythm.

A low growl released from its lips. All the hairs on my neck stood at the sound.

I plunged my hand into my satchel and fumbled for the silver sword. An instinct deep in my core knew the creature had no intention of leaving me alive.

Its twisted lips lifted into a grin as dark as night, and it lunged in a great leap over the grounds.

I yelled as I plunged forward. Rivets of icy air touched my skin as the creature landed behind me, gracefully on all four paws. I pushed up from my knees, the shaking and cold suddenly gone. To kneel would be to die.

My magic pulsed through me. I released a bit and let it lick over the creature's skin. It recoiled at the emptiness. It was neither alive nor dead—and well outside the scope of my powers.

The beast released an eerie sound, half cackle and half howl—laughing at me.

I raised the sword and tried to remember the motions Tyfin had taught me. The lessons blurred in my mind with each sharper pulse of adrenaline.

The shadow creature struck again. It lifted a clawed limb, aiming for my throat. I slid my body back, a simple dodging maneuver, and its claws passed harmlessly in front of my face.

For a moment, a sort of twisted pride expanded in my chest. The beast may kill me, but I learned enough to avoid the first strike. Last time an evil creature attacked me, I'd only watched powerless and fragile, and now my body responded with an innate knowledge of practice and skill.

The pride evaporated quickly as an icy pain cut across my left wrist. I cried out as hot blood swelled to the surface of my skin and that freezing chill sank into my arm. I hadn't moved quite enough to avoid the end of the beast's swipe, and it caught my wrist on the downswing.

Grounding my teeth, the pulsing ache combined with an annoyance with myself. Two steps forward, one step back.

"What do you want?" I asked it, the anger strengthening.

It paused. Its vivid eyes pulsed for a moment, flashing between black and green, before relighting in that fluorescent color again.

My brows creased. Between the flickers of green, it almost looked sad.

But the shadow moved again, a blurred streak in the full darkness as Spirit's Peak had completely claimed the last streaks of sunshine. I held my ground—sword up, preparing for these moments to be my last. I'd try to survive, of course, but held little faith in my nominal swordsman skills.

Its paws beat into the ground. Those glowing eyes fixated on me and promised my death.

I didn't try to dodge it this time. I let the sword swing up, so much lighter and well-balanced compared to the wooden practice blades. It paused at the very top of the arch, fighting against gravity, waiting for my permission to fall again.

The wolf neared. Winter's breath escaped from its body and turned my core cold.

I waited. I had one chance.

Drops of saliva fell from its shadowed maw. It opened its jaws wide, finger-length teeth hidden in the gums.

I let the sword fall. The beast's eyes widened as it calculated the distance between us and realized that it could not avoid my blade completely. Its pace quickened. The strike would land across its front shoulder and wound it, but likely not kill it.

Its teeth cut into my gut the same time my sword found its mark. I gasped as heat and ice blended into my stomach, but a swell of victory emerged at the sight of black smoke leaching from the cut I'd delivered to the creature.

I fell to my knees. The beast circled behind me for another attack—it's final one.

Magic cried inside me, searching for any life or death inside the being that I could manipulate, control. Nothing. It was beyond my abilities.

My fingers shook, slick with my blood, yet I didn't feel afraid. I'd given the beast a good fight. I could die with that.

Its steps beat against the ground. I closed my eyes.

An icy whirl unfolded over my head, followed by a sharp yelp. I tensed, waiting for the pain in the back of my neck as its teeth sliced into me, but nothing came.

Except a soft laugh, a warm one, an annoying familiar one.

I forced my eyes open. A pair of leather-clad legs with worn brown boots met my gaze. The sword dripping black blood at his side was the twin of mine—except larger and longer. I followed the lines of his body up, and up, beyond the stomach and chest I knew were riveted with sharp muscle, to where his stunning face smiled down at me.

Valen.

"Hello, Sunshine," he said, so much promise in those simple words.

My heart thundered again, a new intensity twisting in my core. I missed him, had yearned to see him again.

But I ground my teeth. "What are you doing here?"

"You said 'thank you' wrong." The mercenary wiped the black fluid off his blade on the top of his pants. He slipped it into the sheath at his side.

"I didn't ask for your help."

Valen raised a brow and studied me with cool blue eyes. "I'm sorry. Did you want me to let it kill you?"

"I had it under control."

A smooth smile slipped across his face. I narrowed my eyes. "I can see that."

Valen held out a hand, but I pushed from the ground myself. I forced my knees to stop shaking, refusing to show the man any hint of weakness.

"Leave it to you to fight a Shadow-Beast, Sunshine."

"What's a Shadow-Beast?" I circled the still creature on the ground, more darkness seeping from the cleanly sliced wound Valen's sword inflicted on his neck.

"They're called from the underworld. It takes powerful magic to summon and control one. Few creatures contain the ability, and even fewer humans." He crouched beside it and placed his palm lightly on the body. "It's a shame to kill one. They aren't under their own willpower once summoned. A dark magic, indeed." He looked up at me. "What have you gotten yourself into this time?"

"Me? You're the one intruding on my investigation. *Again.* What are you even doing here?"

Please say you're here for me.

Valen stood, his body fluid and graceful. "You'll be happy to know that it's purely for business purposes. I've been employed to assist the Sheriff's Station with the investigation."

My heart sank more than I'd expected. Of course, the mercenary was here for a job. That's all he cared about.

"Who hired you?"

"I'm not at liberty to say." Valen's gaze softened. He opened his mouth, but only silence flowed out.

My head swam. I sucked in a deep breath. I needed to get to Brew and take a healing tonic, then sleep until my injuries improved.

"Sunshine—"

"My name is Rae," I snapped. "And I don't need your help with the investigation, just like I didn't need you to kill the Shadow-Beast."

A new coldness enveloped me—one I'd long ago recognized as Valen's anger. "I thought you've been training with your sword. You should have been able to handle this."

"I *have* been practicing, but it's only been—Wait! How do you know that? I haven't seen you since solving the Provider's murder." His face pinched for a heartbeat, giving away the secret he tried to hide. "You've been following me? Spying on me?"

Valen sneered. "Don't be ridiculous."

"You have! How else would you know about the training?"

"I—" He paused and looked at me. "Are you ok?"

No, I wasn't. Dizziness stole my vision, and my legs refused to stop shaking. I swayed as the ice in my veins spread deeper from the wounds on my wrist and stomach.

"I'm fine." The air turned thin. My lungs burned. "I don't . . . need you."

My knees buckled. The ground rushed up, stopped only by Valen's arms beneath mine as he caught me.

Darkness swarmed my mind. A quiet calmness whispered sweet nothings in my ear. Sleep would feel so, so good.

Valen's scent of evergreen and summer's breeze infiltrated the drowsiness.

"The hell you don't, Sunshine," he said.

Sleep consumed me.

Chapter 8

I must have passed out in the grass at the college. That explained the rich, earthy scent and an all-consuming flavor of evergreen in my mouth. It didn't quite explain the soft cushioning beneath my body, or the fluff of slick fabric warming my skin.

Maybe I managed to make it to Brew, and it took me home.

Or maybe . . . I didn't think about the other option.

I kept my eyes pinched shut and took an inventory of my body. The shards of ice shredding me from the inside out had faded, replaced with a minor chill and ache. I wiggled my fingers on the injured arm, and they wriggled responsively, though the ache deepened. I was too afraid to move my abdomen yet. That wound had been much harsher.

My magic twisted in my chest. I let it out to touch the space. Its phantom tendrils climbed over every surface in the room and expanded outward, sucking in the life and death of the area. One particular spark tickled the power—something in this house was both alive, yet dead.

I cracked my eyes open. Warm, amber colored wood slants crossed over a vaulted ceiling. Soft torchlight crackled from the walls and cast a comforting glow over the room. Plush rugs consumed dark hardwood floors. Simple cream paint adorned the walls. The wooden bedframe I rested in matched the floors, and the sheets and blanket were solid black.

A white gauze bandage crawled up my arm. Stains of seeping blood and some kind of balm soaked through the wrappings. I assumed my stomach bore a similar treatment.

The masculine feeling of the room combined with the scents told me exactly where I was—someplace I'd never expected: Valen's house. He'd taken me here and tended to my wounds.

As though the man had a direct link to my thoughts, the door slipped open on silent hinges, and he stepped inside with a tray balanced on one hand.

He caught my gaze and paused in the doorway.

"You're awake."

I glanced around the room again. "You took me to your house? Your . . . bedroom?"

He snorted and stepped inside, kicking the door shut with his foot before I could glimpse the adjacent room.

"Don't flatter yourself. This is the guest room." Valen set the tray on the bed beside me. Medical paste, herbal balms, and wrapping supplies littered the surface. He sat on the edge of the mattress beside the tray.

I tried to sit up. As soon as my core tensed, pain and ice ate through my stomach like acid seeping through my veins. I'd accidentally stuck my hand in a pool of Bubbles' acid saliva, which felt mild in comparison. I couldn't muffle the cry that escaped.

Valen firmly pushed me back down. "Relax for five seconds, Sunshine. Nobody recovers that quickly after a Shadow-Beast injury. They tend to turn one's insides into ash."

I clenched my teeth—from both annoyance and pain. "I'd

relax if you'd stop calling me that."

"But it's so fitting for your bright and shining personality."

I hated to admit it, but the familiar banter soothed the ache.

The blanket had slipped to my waist with my movements, exposing the bandaged gut wound at my core. A cool brush of air across my shoulders revealed I wore only my bralette.

"You took my shirt off?" The words sounded more breathless and less snappy than I'd intended. I added a pinched glare to increase the malice.

Valen rolled his eyes. "You almost died, and you're concerned about your modesty? Don't worry, it's nothing I haven't seen before."

I glanced away, hoping he couldn't see the hurt on my face. A memory rose of us sharing a room once, not by my choice, and his exposed chest took my breath away. He seemed to find more words as he saw more of me.

Good. That was *good*. Valen was nobody—nothing to me.

The mercenary lifted my arm and gently placed it across his knees. The cool leather mixed with heat from his body. I bit my lip. His fingertips ran along the end of the bandage, lifting one corner.

"I can tend to my own wounds."

"Oh, really?" He leaned back. "Go ahead."

I ground my teeth, the pain of moving moments ago, still fresh in my mind.

"That's what I thought."

Valen removed the soiled bandages with unexpected care. He lifted my arm toward the candlelight, his fingers a feather's touch on my damaged skin. The wound looked good: no pus or streaks to indicate infection.

"This wound looks great," he said. "I think it will heal well."

I smiled.

"What's that look for?" He dabbed some kind of clear fluid onto a cotton wad and tapped it against the gash.

"Sometimes I wonder if you can read my mind," I said. Maybe the fading adrenaline or near-death experience made me feel bold.

He didn't glance up from my arm. "Maybe we're more connected than you want to realize."

"I doubt that. People from . . . my previous life made sure all my connections were severed."

"And where was that previous life, Sunshine?"

I looked away from him to study the ceiling. "Far away, where the word sunshine wasn't on anyone's mind. Only survival." Erline had been a special place, filled with torture and despair. The capital took me as a young child to serve the king with my magic—and he demanded all from his Providers.

If the king ever found me, he would take me back to the capital and make me long for death.

"What about you?" I asked. "I thought you'd fled Hallow's Promise, but it turns out you have a house, and a *guest room*."

He laughed softly. "Maybe I come from somewhere without sunshine too, and it's hard to leave now that I've found some."

When I looked back, Valen stared at me. His crystal eyes sank into my soul, trying to untangle all my secrets, even the ones I didn't know about.

"How did you get out?" he whispered. "From the darkness."

I swallowed. I'd only ever told Krissa the truth about my escape from Erline, and only after several glasses of wine and magic brew. She knew about Brew's true origin—that my necromantic power had instilled sentience into the wagon— and that I was once a Provider.

"I did terrible things. Mostly to terrible people, but not all . . . not all of them were terrible." I'd used my magic to give one man the lives of four people—too much life and power for an individual to sustain. I'd used him, and left him at the capital's gates, knowing he'd perish from the onslaught of power.

"How many people did you kill to escape, Rae?"

The mercenary's gaze was a spell over me, one without a drop of magic. I knew that look, the look of death, and being the reason behind it. Valen had certainly killed people in his profession, probably more than I had.

"Five. I killed five people before I came to Hallow's Promise."

His eyes clouded, memories overwhelming him too. "Are you sure about that?"

"I—Ahhh." I groaned as I shifted too fast. The wound in my gut pulsed with pain, bright and cold and consuming.

"Shhhh." He eased the bandages from my core. "Let me tend to this, and it'll feel better."

A fresh bandage wrapped over my arm. I hadn't noticed, but the subtle ache *had* faded. Valen knew what he was doing with the herbs and balms.

I arched my neck to study the gash while he dabbed the liquid over it. Rows of deep gouges ran parallel before slashing downward, where the Shadow-Beast's long teeth sank into my flesh. I wondered if Valen had seen my organs before patching me up and locked that thought deep into the back of my mind.

"Here." The mercenary paused his work to hand me a glass with a hollow reed haphazardly resting on the side. "I also brought you tea."

"You?" I let the disbelief color my voice. "Made tea?"

"Of course not. I'd never stoop so low. I bought it from the market earlier, before unexpectedly having to rescue you."

"You didn't rescue me," I mumbled, but sipped the drink through the reed, anyway. It was surprisingly good, a blend of simple black tea with notes of honey and something slightly bitter. "You distracted me from my fight."

"I distracted you from dying," he said. Valen smoothed a light balm over the cuts and set a fresh bandage on top. "Now don't move too much because I can't wrap this around your torso yet. Which shouldn't be a problem, since you'll be asleep soon, anyway."

I creased my brows. "I don't have time to sleep. I need take Brew downtown before the supper rush, and also see if Leof's gotten a response from the magic cast expert yet."

Valen stood. He carefully and slowly packed all the supplies onto the tray. "Well, all of that's going to be hard, seeing as I just drugged you."

"What?" The tea, that damned tea. I should have recognized the bitterness of henbane hidden beneath the honey. I tried to sit up. The wound hurt, but my limbs grew heavy, and my neck didn't want to support my head. "Why?"

"You need to rest, Sunshine, and you seem to be incapable of it any other way. Don't worry, I'll try to protect your modesty while you sleep."

I'm pretty sure he winked at me as he shut the door with a soft click, but my vision twisted with the drug.

My head fell into the pillow. When I woke up, I'd do something . . . something terrible . . . to someone . . . someone . . . somewhere . . .

Chapter 9

My head pounded. Pulsing aches throbbed through my body with every beat of my heart. The wounds felt better than they had earlier, in Valen's house—

I jerked upright. My vision spun with the henbane remnants, but I recognized the space immediately. Brew vibrated lightly beneath me. I sat on the wagon's floor, where the hard wood had somehow softened under me, and a low flame on the stove heated the air. The rear door was latched from the inside.

"You let him in?" I asked the wagon.

It creaked, a mild complaint.

"What have I told you about strangers?"

A puff popped from one of the herb containers, releasing a soft shower of dried turmeric.

"Very mature." Golden powder stuck to my hair. "But you know that man is dangerous. You need to be careful."

Brew snapped a cupboard closed. I sighed and pushed up from the floor. A thin linen blanket pooled at my feet with an unwelcome, earthy smell. My shirt had been returned, complete with the new slashes slicing the fabric over my stomach. I lifted the hem. White bandages wrapped around my abdomen, holding the salve in place.

I'd almost died. As much as I hated admitting it, Valen had saved my life, then tended to me. He brought me here because he knew I'd be safe with Brew.

I ran my hand along Brew's smooth countertop. "Thank you for keeping me safe while I . . . rested."

A series of happy pulses buzzed up my feet.

The wards tapped softly in my mind. Someone was on my property, but the protections remained intact. A slow smile spread across my lips. Valen would have broken my wards if he could have, just to prove his almighty ego. Resorting to laying me in the wagon meant he felt the new and improved spells. Bummer, I wanted to see the Lightning-Crotch in action.

I squinted as light flooded my eyes when I opened the door. The lingering headache from the drug hurt more than the Shadow-Beast wounds. Valen had done a good job with whatever healing tonics he used—not that I'd ever tell the mercenary that.

Krissa stood from a white rocking chair she'd added to my porch after we'd become friends. She held an envelope over her eyes to shield them from the afternoon sun.

All night—I'd spent the whole night at Valen's house, and half the day sleeping off the drug he'd slipped me. Next time I saw the man, he'd suffer the consequences.

"You look like a wagon ran you over, then went back and did it again," Krissa said as I staggered across the short path from Brew to the porch.

I gave her a stern look up and down. "That means a lot, coming from you."

Krissa glanced down at her dress, filled with creases and wrinkles. Two different socks stretched to her knees, each a more vivid rainbow pattern than the other. Her hair, normally pressed into neat braids with woven ribbon, piled haphazardly on top of her head.

She grimaced. "It's been a rough couple of days, but I'm not the one who was sleeping in a wagon."

"I'll give you one chance to guess why I was in there."

Her nose pinched right at the center. "Valen. He's back?"

I nodded. "Someone hired him to help investigate the case. He won't say who."

"Great."

I reached for the knob, my wards easing as they recognized me. Krissa caught my wrist, carefully avoiding the bandages.

"What's this?"

"I may have also been attacked at the college. Valen called it a Shadow-Beast."

Krissa arched her brows. "Those are very rare."

"Apparently I'm lucky."

The door opened and a rush of security covered me as I stepped inside the cottage. It wasn't a large space. The living room and kitchen covered the downstairs, while a ladder led to a little loft where my bed stayed. The murderer of my last case had broken into my home and wrecked the place. I'd carefully put it back together, piece by piece, with Krissa and Leof's help. Friends, it turned out, help each other.

"Do you think Magnolia's killer summoned the Shadow-Beast?"

"It seems like too much of a coincidence for the events to be unconnected." I pulled a mug from the counter and poured some goat's milk into the bottom. Flames rose in the fire as I perched the cauldron on the hook.

Krissa sat on the couch. Bubbles, who hadn't even moved at my entrance, blinked his little eyes open from the adjacent cushion. He flicked his long tongue over both eyes before hopping onto the professor's lap. He went limp as Krissa ran her hand over his back.

"But she was killed with magic, not attacked by a creature."

I retrieved the mortar and pestle from the cupboard and set it on the large table near the stove. I'd never eaten a meal at the table—it was reserved for potion and product preparation.

"Whoever's responsible for this has access to different types of magic and isn't afraid to experiment with them."

"They could be channeling power from something else."

I snapped a piece of fresh ginger from a larger root and used the edge of a small knife to peel away the skin. It clunked to the bottom of the mortar, joined by a healthy dose of peppermint, the strongest black tea in my collection, and a sprinkle of valerian root. I ground the pestle into the marble. The stones ground against each other, emitting a horrible noise from the bowl. I didn't stop. I needed the tea to revive me. Once a fine powder replaced the herbs, I dumped the mixture into the warming milk over the flames.

"Oh, I almost forgot. A messenger dropped off this letter for you." Krissa held out the envelope she'd used as a shade cover earlier. A red wax seal covered the envelope flap, with a simple "F" embellishing the stamp.

I accepted the letter and peeled open the envelope.

To the Hallow's Promise Crime Investigation Expert:

Greetings from afar.

My name is Fraya Gernstart Hawkthorne, and I am writing in response to an inquiry from Marshal Leof (. I've been requested to perform a magic cast analysis and comparison regarding a murder at the Central Campus of Mages and Magic.

I have made myself present in the local area and am willing to meet on the second weekday at 8:00pm at the intersection of Oath Street and Honor Way.

With kind regards.

Fraya

"Who's it from?"

I folded the letter and stuffed it back in the envelope. "The magic cast expert. She wants to meet me on Oath and Honor tonight."

Krissa's brows creased. "The Chopines? Gross."

I nodded and stirred the brewing tea. The southern tip of Hallow's Promise housed the most wealthy and extravagant, who tried to avoid the rest of the town at all costs. Officially called Glory's Gardens, Hallow's Promise residents nicknamed the area The Chopines, after an incredibly ridiculous shoe rich women wore to avoid stepping in mud—which assumed the rest of us were the mud.

I removed a small bowl, filled it halfway with more milk, and spooned thick globs of golden honey into the liquid. I used a flat whisk to spin the two together, expanding the fats in the milk until a heavy froth clung to the metal. The herbs would be enough to curb the headache, but I also wanted the tea to taste good.

"I'll go with you," Krissa said.

I carefully pulled the cauldron from the fire and tipped the spouted edge into my cup.

"I don't know if that's the best idea," I said, slowly. Feelings of guilt pinched in my chest as the words came out.

She crossed her arms. "Why not?"

"Well, you're sort of under investigation for the murder. Any evidence I find exonerating you would hold more weight if you weren't involved."

She bit her lip. "I guess that makes sense. They are sort of searching my house right now."

A red haze snapped over my vision and the headache grew worse.

"What?"

She shrugged, but a slight shake went through her shoulders. She was scared. "It's not a surprise. They're looking to see if there's evidence I hired someone to kill Magnolia. They won't find anything, obviously."

That explained the wrinkled dress and half-finished hairstyle. They'd probably pulled her out of her house with little warning.

"Castor," I said, not a question. My hands balled into tight fists, and I saw his death in my mind. The king be damned. I'd kill the constable for hurting my friend like this.

Krissa lifted Bubbles from her lap to the next cushion, rose from the couch, and stood beside me. She didn't look at me as she scooped the honey-foam onto the top of my tea, grabbed my hands, and pressed the warm mug into them.

"Maybe you should drink some of this."

I put the cup to my lips, half dazed with anger. Warm, rich tea flooded my mouth, sweet but earthy from the goat's milk. The herbs and hint of magic in the potion eased the anger slightly, enough to revive some coherent thoughts.

"Thank you," I murmured. "Do you want some?"

"Some goat milk tea? Yuck, no thanks. I *was* hoping I could spend another night here, though? I don't . . . I don't want to go home until they're all done."

I took another big drink and set the glass down. I bundled Krissa into my arms and squeezed her close to me. She hesitated for a moment—probably surprised by the rare burst of affection—then hugged me back.

"You can stay as long as you want," I said.

She pulled back. "Is that a good idea? I don't want anyone to think I'm meddling in the investigation."

"You're my friend." The simple words answered everything.

Krissa squeezed my hand, and we perched on the couch while I finished my tea and talked about anything besides the case.

Chapter 10

My skin itched every time I entered The Chopines. Neat rows of matching houses, perfectly balanced between welcoming and arrogant, lined the squared streets. The cobblestones had been ground flat, so wagons passing over the surface didn't feel the slightest bump. It seemed even the fauna were groomed into submission as beautifully colored birds fluttered through the sky like ribbons of rainbow.

It made my jaw clench.

I had known plenty of wealthy people at the capital—far above anyone that would settle in Hallow's Promise. Most of them used layers of expensive perfume to hide the sharp stench of rot from the inside out.

Blooming jasmine bushes lined the intersection of Oath Street and Honor Way. The leaves of the delicate plant were expertly trimmed to drape onto the road, avoiding any possible damage from a runaway wagon.

I ground my heel into one of the lower leaves. A guilty satisfaction warmed my gut at the imprint of my sole in the plant. As lowly as I was, I had left a mark on this place.

"You must be Rae." A woman stepped from the shadows, followed by a large bird-like creature with vivid rich feathers the color of fresh blood. The animal rose almost to her waist, with sharp eyes and an even sharper beak. It kept a step behind her, attached by a thick leather leash, one eye on its owner and the other on me.

"Fraya?" I asked, though who else could the stranger from the shadows be?

She offered her hand flatly, as royalty might approach a commoner. I gripped her fingertips awkwardly, but didn't raise them to my lips. I'd utilize my new sword skills before I kissed another hand.

"It's a delight," she almost purred, unflustered by my reaction. "I was quite glad to receive the marshal's letter. I imagine magic cast comparison experts are rather difficult to come by." Fraya offered me her arm. "Please, let's walk."

Fraya's gray hair wrapped into a tight bun atop her head. Rows of simple braids circled the knot. She smelled a little like lemon, and a little like a fresh wood mill. She set a steady pace, followed by me, then the bird creature on its leash.

She caught my gaze as I glanced at the being again.

"No need to fret. He's harmless."

I offered a small smile but had a terrible mental image of Bubbles being swallowed in one gulp. I was glad I'd left him with Krissa at home.

"Tell me, how are you able to perform a magic cast?"

I pressed my lips. I didn't have much experience working with comparison experts, but I'd expected her to ask about the case first, not me.

"I'm a witch," I said—which was mostly true. "I was able to force the magic residue to soak into the casting material."

"A witch? Any particular kind?"

"A normal kind, I'm afraid." The lies were so familiar now,

they didn't even taste bitter.

Fraya drew us to a halt before a sizeable residence, edged in marble trim, and lined with golden stamps pressed into the brick walkway.

The intensity of her dark eyes drew me in as she gazed into my face.

"You are never normal," she almost whispered. "Remember that."

The woman dropped my arm and turned onto the path before my thoughts caught up. I followed her, mouth slightly open, words completely faded from my mind.

The oak door opened with the lightest touch of Fraya's hand. More marble tumbled across the floor, etching into a brilliant mosaic of blues and whites in the very center. A twisting staircase lined the side of the space and disappeared into an upper story. Most torches remained unlit, allowing the few flames to awash the room in heated gold.

"You . . . live here?" Ah, my ability to speak returned which such eloquent diction.

Fraya paused and glanced around. Her eyes widened as she took in the lavish furniture, the careful artworks perched on the walls. When she looked back at me, a smug smile lifted half of her lips.

"I'm staying here—for a while, at least, if the accommodations continue to please me."

I probably looked like a fish gasping for water. Any sane person would describe the home as overwhelming and beautiful. Fraya must set very high expectations for her arrangements.

"Please, sit. I'll check for refreshments."

Fraya gestured to a deep blue velvet couch and disappeared toward the back, where I assumed a kitchen must be.

I sat on the edge of the couch. I worried some dust or lingering herbs would stain the fine fabric.

My discomfort grew the longer Fraya took. The dancing torchlight seemed to whisper at me in the dimness. *You don't belong. You never have. You never will.* Normally, I understood the shadows and their muttered words, but tonight they rang too close to the truth. This finery, this wealth, would never be me.

But I had something better now—friends.

Fraya's steps echoed across the tiles as she appeared empty-handed. "So sorry, it appears the kitchen is not as well-stocked as anticipated." She smoothed her silk dress beneath her legs as she sat on a chair across from me. The bird settled over his feet. Those sharp eyes locked on me.

"Tell me about the magic you used to create the cast," Fraya said.

I raised my brow. "Wouldn't you like to know about the patterns observed in the cast? I've heard you can find possible magic types even without a standard to compare to?"

Fraya waved my words away. "Yes, yes, we'll have plenty of time to talk about that, but I need to know how the cast was made, in case it causes any imperfections."

I kept the snide thoughts to myself. "It was a simple infusion of magic that allowed the foreign power to soak into the casting powder, creating a pattern specific to that individual. Any witch with the knowledge could do it."

"Where did you apply the powder?"

"It covered the body and . . . do you want to hear more about the scene?"

She tapped her chin. "No, I don't think that would benefit me. How were you able to sense the lingering magic in the first place?"

"I don't understand how this will help in your comparison?"

"I'm simply curious. It's quite unusual to perform a magic cast in an actual murder. I'd like to learn as much as possible for the future."

I nodded, my confusion eased a bit. The discipline was rather rare. It was logical that Fraya wanted to learn more about my methods to pass them along to future inspectors.

I summarized my methods and brought up some of the literature I'd studied to learn the craft. When I finished, Fraya smiled wider than she had all night.

She leaned back in her chair. "Thank you for the information, Rae. I'll be in touch to schedule some time to review the cast you've collected."

"What?" I wanted to poke my finger in my ears, in case something stuck inside made me hear her wrong. "You don't want to talk about the case or the cast at all? What about timeline expectations or payments?"

"I believe the Marshal will take care of those details. Now that I'm satisfied the cast is well made, I am willing to examine it. I'll be in touch—as I've said."

I heard the dismissal in her voice. Part of me protested as I stood from the velvet seat, but I bit my tongue. I had limited choices, and Krissa's innocence was on the line.

Fraya didn't stand as I walked to the door. Soft clips of talons on tiles echoed as the bird creature followed me out.

"Have a good night, Rae," she called after me. "Please close the door behind you."

I nodded. The red bird stopped before the doorway. He caught my gaze. Our eyes locked, a harshness in those sharp avian eyes. It felt like he tried to say something through the dark orbs, but I couldn't understand the flashes of reflecting flames or too-long blinks.

"I'm sorry," I whispered. *I'm sorry I don't understand you or know what you want me to do.*

I closed the door until the latch clicked.

Chapter 11

Downtown Hallow's Promise drew the most visitors than any other part of town. Taverns and inns lined the street, nestled among markets and little shops in-between. Visitors weren't always the best customers for me—few understood my products enough to buy them. But I needed money and to make progress on this case, so Brew parked us across the street from the Sheriff's Station. I planned to catch Leof before he went home for the day.

Maybe it was the warm air, or the gossip about the murder at the college, but a line spilled from Brew's window onto the edge of the street.

"Tell me about the creature again." Krissa leaned against the counter while I worked on a drink order.

"It was a big, red bird. It didn't do anything." I didn't mention the almost desperate attempt at communication we'd shared during my departure. Krissa hadn't been my friend long enough to see all my crazy thoughts.

"And she didn't say anything about the magic cast?"

I shook my head. "Nothing. It was . . . really strange."

"Well, you were in The Chopines." She shivered, and Brew sent a sympathetic warm breeze through the wagon. Krissa smiled and affectionately patted the counter.

"That's true."

The bell outside the wooden sash dinged, and Krissa returned to the window.

"Another chilled Par-Tea, please!"

I wiped a bead of sweat from my forehead as I prepared the drink. I pried a lid from a new jar of apple cider vinegar and stuck a spoon in for a quick taste-test. The concoction had been fermenting for over two months in Brew's cupboard. The rich natural sweetness of the apples blended with the sharp vinegar bite. Perfect.

I added a few spoonfuls of the mix into a glass. The amber liquid clinging to the side washed away as I poured in water mixed with molasses. I'd frothed a mixture of more molasses and sweet cream, which I topped onto the drink.

"Par-Tea, ready to go." I handed the drink over, and Krissa passed it to the customer. The Par-Tea was a custom derivative of Switchel, a beverage known to promote hydration and energy. As soon as the customer wobbled away, the bell tolled again.

"Another," Krissa said.

I repeated the drink again and again, and she passed them through the window. I let my mind wander as the sun sank lower, and the crowd thinned.

The murderer must be involved with the college. They may have a personal vendetta against Magnolia, sure, but the Shadow-Beast attack also occurring on campus meant they knew I was there. They would be familiar enough that their presence wasn't suspicious to anyone else.

"Rae." Krissa tapped my arm. I jumped. "Sorry. I called you a few times, but you weren't answering."

"No problem. I got lost in my thoughts. What do you need?"

She gestured to the sash. "This customer says they have something to tell you."

I put down the grater and half-shredded ginger root. A pitcher of water perched beside a copper basin on the counter, and I rinsed my hands before leaning out the window.

A young man casually stood outside. He dug his hands deep into his trouser pockets. He wore a black cloak over a black tunic, giving me a momentary flashback to when I once wore a similar cloak—with the addition of a veiled hood hiding my face.

I sucked in a breath. He wasn't a Provider. He looked like a normal young man.

"Can I help you?" I asked. "We have a menu, but I can make custom drinks too."

He glanced over his shoulder before stepping closer to Brew and leaning into the window. I kept the smile on my face, even though I hated when people did that. Brew creaked, sensing my displeasure.

"I need to tell you something about Professor Galrod's murder," he said.

I tensed and glanced at Krissa. She raised her brows up and down, not even trying to suppress the smile on her face.

"What's your name?" I asked.

The man shook his head. "If anyone knew I came here, it would put my attendance at the college in danger. The dean has forbidden anyone to speak to investigators, at risk of expulsion. My name doesn't matter, anyway, only what I know."

Dean Perthum had a secret so deep, he'd forbidden students to mention it to the constables? I had to know.

"Tell me," I whispered, putting the barest touch of magic into the words. Not enough to steal his will, but to entice him a bit.

"Before Professor Galrod's death, another instructor went missing. She still hasn't returned, and there's been an adjunct teaching her classes for over a week."

"Who?"

"Professor Irabel Wulfclad Ironhand. She taught Intro to Magical Healing." The boy's lip quivered. "I thought . . . someone should know about her."

I wanted to touch his hand, but didn't think he would appreciate the gesture. "Thank you for telling me. You did the right thing. Here, let me get you something."

I dipped back inside the wagon. Brew pulled open the cupboard before I asked. A row of pre-made juices sat on one shelf, and I found a subtle spearmint green tea, good for relaxing the nerves.

"Here." I passed the drink along. "And thank you again."

The man remained silent as he tipped his head, tucked the sealed jar against his chest, and disappeared into the night.

I slammed the sash down. Brew was closed for the night.

"Did you hear that?" I whispered, even though the wagon would prevent any unwanted ears from listening.

Krissa nodded, bouncing on her toes in excitement. "Yes, Irabel has gone missing, and the dean is preventing students from mentioning anything!"

"Don't sound too excited. Did you know she was missing?"

"Sorry." She stopped jumping quite so high. "No, but I wouldn't have known. She worked in another department than my statistics class, a whole different wing actually. But why would Perthum want to keep it secret? I mean, I hope Irabel is found safe, of course, but it's suspicious!"

I nodded, but didn't say anything. It certainly *was* suspicious.

"I need to go across the street and talk to Leof. Are you alright waiting in here?"

"Are you going to tell him about Irabel?"

"Yes."

"Then I'll wait right here, and try to contain my excitement, and hope nothing bad happened to her. But also, I hope that this gets Castor off my back."

I left the wagon and waited for the latch to click behind me, wishing all the same things too.

* * *

Leof's office was bigger than mine. If I had a larger ego, I would have been jealous, but I'd sat in one of the plush chairs before the fireplace and watched Leof piece together one mystery after another. He deserved the big office.

Tonight, the oil in the lamps ran low. A flickering shadow danced on the walls as the wicks desperately attempted to stay lit. Leof perched at the desk pushed along the left side of the room, where he only worked when he was really desperate.

He glanced at me, hints of werewolf gold in his iris. "I should have known you'd show up."

I pushed one of the heavy chairs to face his desk and plopped into the seat. The cushion greeted me warmly.

"Apparently, I don't have anything better to do than work for you."

The marshal laughed. "You don't have anyone else to bother, you mean?"

I smiled, but it felt thin. Leof and Valen didn't exactly get along, and bringing up the mercenary's timely return could drastically shorten one of their lifespans.

"How's Suzie?" I softened my voice. Leof's daughter was also a sensitive topic.

He shrugged, but a sigh escaped at the same time. "She's been making some new friends at River's Edge." The town beside Hallow's Promise, which also shared the other side of Spirit's Peak. "I'm not sure it's a good thing."

"They're rowdy?" Suzie had a good head on her shoulders, mostly from her dad's examples of hard work and perseverance. I couldn't see her falling into a bad crowd.

"They're . . . high class."

I raised my brows.

Leof waved the expression away. "I know that shouldn't mean anything. But they have higher standards, and I'm worried how Suzie will handle the pressure. Especially since we . . . aren't financially comparable." Living off a marshal's salary didn't open the doors to any class promotions. "Her mother's thrilled, of course."

She would be. Kara—Leof's ex—measured success in coins, and joy in other people's pain.

"Suzie's smart. She'll make the right choices, but even if she doesn't, she's all grown up now. You have let her make her own mistakes."

The wolf grunted. "Did you forget who you're talking to? Why are you even here this late?"

"I met with the magic cast expert."

"And?" Leof didn't try to hide the spark of excitement on his face. Investigators loved new clues in a case.

"And nothing, yet. I'm hoping she'll have more when she sees the cast." I opened my mouth to say more—maybe mention the strange bird, or Fraya's impressive accommodations—but a flash of yellow light bounced against a glass on Leof's desk. The cluster of gray hairs I'd collected at the scene perched inside. They looked soft, almost fluffy and light.

"Did you scent map that?" I asked.

"Huh? Oh." Leof picked up the jar and held it out to me. I stood from the chair to accept the evidence. "Yeah, I did. Not too much information about the source, but if I smell it again, I'll recognize it right away."

Leof shuffled through the pages on his desk and handed me a transcribed copy of his notes:

Overall: Gray or off-white, fine or feather-like texture
Origins: Unknown—nonhuman
Notes: Distinct hints of fruit and meat. Potential omnivorous creature. Fresh underlying scent—rain, water, moisture of some sort.
Certainty Level: 4

"The certainty level is pretty high," I said. It was an estimate of how likely Leof could identify the scent if presented with it again, presented on a scale of 1 to 5.

He leaned back on his chair. "It's a distinct scent. It made a good map. Now, I'd like to get home and have some food before you start looking like a steak dinner. Did you only come here to check on Suzie and insult me?"

"No. Find a snack because you can't eat me before I finish talking." I flopped back onto the chair and settled in for a long discussion. "Let me fill you in about Professor Irabel Ironhand."

* * *

"I don't understand why *that* creature needs to be at this meeting." Dean Perthum raised his upper lip in Bubbles' direction. The warplog sprawled on his back across my lap, his mouth half open and his round tummy exposed to the world. Both of his rabbit-like hind legs draped off my knees and his tiny front feet fell to each side.

Bubbles was at the meeting because he'd devoured half of a rotting cow this morning, and if I left him unsupervised, he'd regurgitate the bones and gnaw them to shards all over Brew or my house. The gnawing kept his rapidly growing teeth at a reasonable length, but I tried to limit it to smaller meals so I had less stinky bone fragments littering my floor.

I didn't tell Perthum any of that. Instead, I clutched the creature a little closer, to which he released a slight burp, and smiled.

"I have the discretion to investigate this case the way I see fit, and Bubbles is a necessary part of my process."

Bub gave a sleepy hiccup in agreement.

"Continuing," Perthum said, his gaze still seething in my direction. "You had questions about Irabel's disappearance."

The dean's office wasn't as large as Leof's, but matched his attire more fittingly. Dark mahogany bookshelves contained the perfect balance of books and nick-nacks to appear studious and not cluttered. Deep purple cushions balanced against a bench along a sweeping tall window, where the morning sun turned rainbow through stained glass. To Perthum's left was another door, shut tight.

Leof crossed his arms. The gesture made his muscles appear larger and more menacing. The dean tried not to stare, but his throat bobbed.

"Why did you keep that information to yourself?"

Perthum snorted. "Information? There is no information about Irabel leaving this campus. She'd considered quitting several times before."

"Did she get along with Magnolia?"

He cut that gaze back to me. "Magnolia was sharp and cunning. She had a lot of knowledge and enjoyed passing that along. But she wasn't particularly well liked. I received several complaints every semester, describing her as difficult to work with. So no, Irabel and Magnolia didn't really 'get along.'"

"Did she have anything in common with Magnolia? Were they part of the same professional organizations or friend circles?"

When I felt angry, heat encompassed my body from the inside out. Valen eluded an icy chill palpable from a distance. Dean Perthum's anger, however, felt sharp and crystalline. Thick wads of glass attempted to slice at me.

But Perthum didn't know my magic mingled with the dead, and we felt no pain.

I kept my face flat. After a moment, the man leaned back in his chair, a whiff of mothballs blurting from his dark robes.

"What do you know about the Board of Professional Standards?" he asked.

I tried to keep my eyes from widening. It certainly wasn't the question I'd expected. I had a vague memory of Krissa mentioning it days ago, but I couldn't quite capture the details.

"Not much," I admitted.

"The Board of Professional Standards is the front face of a much larger, more secret organization. Each college must submit one professor to serve on the board. They indulge in secret magical research, determining which can be publicized and taught, and which are too . . . vile to exist beyond the theoretical. It's a great honor to be on the board, but also a burden, for family and friends can never know the details of such an organization." Perthum paused for a heartbeat. "But they compensate for that burden by offering a single representative each year one fulfilled wish of their choice."

I raised my brows. "There's over a hundred colleges across Erline's rule. The likelihood of having a wish granted is minimal."

"I don't disagree." Perthum nodded. "But many compete for a spot on the Board to even attempt to gain their wish. That is why Magnolia's retirement was so sought after. Her space would be opened for a new member. Irabel was among the many that longed for such an advantage."

Magnolia's death suddenly made more sense. Not only was she disliked among the school, but she held an opportunity for a very coveted gift. Granting wishes was not an easy magic, nor a particularly predictable one. It couldn't kill or bestow life, but it did promise very immense rewards.

I rubbed my fingers over Bub's belly. The soft up and down of each breath comforted me.

Krissa had wanted Magnolia's position on the Board. That meant she likely had a wish she wanted to be granted. What could it be?

I pushed the personal thoughts aside. Magnolia's murder needed to be my focus now. "Would anyone else want the position?"

"Only every professor on this campus, including me, if administration were eligible to serve. Now, I'm growing tired of these questions. Irabel is not missing, she's likely throwing another one of her tantrums and will either return or finally resign. If that is all, you two are dismissed from my office."

Perthum grabbed a handful of pages and shuffled them, though I knew he couldn't be reading anything.

"You don't have a problem with us searching Irabel's office, then?" Leof asked.

A loud bang erupted against the door to Perthum's left. The man didn't acknowledge the sound, but shadows danced beneath the door.

Perthum waved his hand at us. "I don't care at all. The guards will tell me when you finally depart."

Leof stood, but a subtle growl followed another bang against the door. Bubbles flicked his eyes open and waved his little feet until I flipped him onto this stomach. He licked one of his eyes, but a drip of acid saliva conjugated on the edge of his lips.

"What's behind the door?" I asked.

"Really?" Perthum slammed his pages down, the rattle of desk half covering another crash against the wood. "Do you have no sense of personal privacy? I dare say—"

The dean didn't finish his sentence before the door splintered from the hinges. I hunched over Bubbles and covered my eyes as shards spread over us. A moment later, Bubbles jumped from my lap and an eerie growl slipped through the room.

I rubbed dust out of my eyes, revealing another creature sniffing Bubbles' flat nose. It resembled a cat and a monkey, sort of hunched over with a wickedly long tail. Its two front paws gripped the warplog's face and sucked in a deep breath.

A fine, downy fur covered it's body.

I jumped up, ready to defend Bubbles if the beast made one wrong move. "What is that?"

Perthum stood too, his face red. "It's a harloon. It's mine, and it is certainly not relevant to your case." He pointed one shaking finger at us. "Now take your ugly, giant frog and GET OUT!"

I cast a side glance at Leof. I knew he was also thinking about the hairs found beneath Magnolia's body. "Can you get the scent from here?"

He shook his head. "Too many interferences."

I swung back to Perthum. "We'll need a fur sample from your harloon."

"You . . . you'll . . . you want . . ." A chuckle slipped from the Dean's lips. All the prestige and poise fell apart like an egg scrambled in a pan. He straightened his shoulders, raised his hands, and magic as sharp as his anger boiled through the room. "You will leave now, or you will not have any LEGS TO LEAVE ON!"

I didn't ask twice. I snatched Bubbles where he purred in the harloon's grip, and Leof and I bolted out the door. The lock snapped on its own the moment we'd left.

Leof stretched his neck. "I think that went well."

I gasped for air. My head hurt from the tension and seeing Bubbles near a creature that may or may not be involved in a murder.

A murder where Krissa was the prime suspect.

"Do you think we can still search Irabel's office?" Leof asked, not sucking in air the way I did.

"I can't . . ." I panted. "I . . . have a party . . . tonight."

Leof didn't bother hiding his eye roll. "Fine, I'll do it myself."

Chapter 12

The Shrine District sat awkwardly between Main Street and the wealthier parts of Hallow's Promise. Respectable families lived there, with simple, well-built homes and steady incomes, even if occasionally questionable. The streets were clean, the nights were quiet, and the hazy stench of booze from downtown only drifted through on particularly windy days.

They also knew how to throw a party.

Pulses of magically enhanced music beat through the ground from a cluster of musicians across the courtyard, vibrating Brew's floorboards. The wagon itself seemed to pulse with the rhythm, its own kind of dancing. People moved through the fading light as the long summer day succumbed to night.

A cluster of three young women walked toward Brew's sash, their faces shadowed as they peered over their shoulders and whispered.

"Is that really him?" One woman stared into the crowd, and I tracked her gaze. Across the way, surrounded by a group of well-dressed people, a man with a thin goatee and dark hair tipped his head back. A deep-throated laugh caught in the wind and echoed all the way to us.

"I can't believe he came to a *party*. Should he even be here?

It's so tasteless," the second girl asked, a slight slur to her words. She giggled and stepped into the torchlight spilling from the wagon. Her eyes narrowed as she squinted to study the menu. "I'll have the Mug Shot, please."

Curiosity burned me as I returned a smile to the customer and nodded. I rarely added alcohol to my beverages, and she probably didn't need another drink, but I was hired to be at the party and, well, a party was a party.

The trio continued to whisper as I set a small mug on my cutting board. Brew popped open the herb cupboard overhead. I shuffled out a few sprigs of rosemary and set one against the flames of the oven beside me.

The dried leaves caught fire, and I knew the floral, earthy scent of rosemary spread from the wagon, but I'd made the drink so many times tonight, I didn't smell it anymore. I shook my hand hard enough to extinguish the flame and dropped the smoldering stick into the mug.

I didn't *really* want to eavesdrop on my customers. But it wasn't my fault when they laughed and giggled so close to Brew's sash.

"Do you think he did it?" the first girl asked.

I pressed my lips. The pre-made rosemary syrup waited beside me, but I plucked the thicker rose syrup from its place on the counter. It wouldn't alter the flavor of the drink, but added a lovely pink tint the woman probably couldn't see.

"Professor Dominic?" The third woman snorted, an oddly familiar edge to the sound. "He doesn't have the balls to kill anyone."

"Ugh!" My hand slipped at the name, spilling a generous helping of bright pink liquid into the bottom of the mug.

Professor Dominic? Magnolia's previous relationship? Here?

Now?

I gulp, dragging a wet towel blindly over the counter and stood on my tiptoes to get a better look at Dominic. He held a wineglass in one manicured hand, lifting it toward the perfectly groomed facial hair below his lip. His maroon jacket buttoned to the top of his chest, where a black silk handkerchief peeked out.

I needed to talk to him.

The third voice interrupted my search. "Excuse me, my friend's waiting for her drink—Oh. It's you."

Suzie, Leof's daughter, scowled at me. A wildfire of embers lit inside her eyes as dislike rose to the surface. I hadn't seen her since a threat from my past appeared at her father's doorstep and injured him—badly. Suzie was more than human, and though I'd never seen her shapeshift like her father, I knew fire ran in her veins.

"Hi Suzie." I forced a smile. "Sorry about that. I'll finish the drink right away. Can I start anything for you?"

That heated gaze dropped to my hands, like my touch may soil her beverage. "No. Thanks."

I started the drink again, lighting a new spring of rosemary and dropping it into a new cup. I tried to be casual, uninterested, cool.

"So, uh, who's that guy?" I shrugged toward Dominic.

Suzie rolled her eyes. I braced myself for the harsh comment, but one of her friends cut in before she launched them at me.

The girl put her hand on the sash and dropped her voice. "That's Professor Dominic. He teaches Wild History, if you know what I mean" I certainly did not know what she meant. "But his ex just got *murdered,* and *he* probably did it."

"Hmmm," I said. The rose syrup clung to the edges just

right this time. I added the rosemary and two flavors of booze into a larger glass. The barley-based alcohol was commonly sold from any local vendor, but the alcohol in the tall, slim green bottle was brewed by seclusive communities in the Far Mountains. They sent people twice per year on each solstice to sell their wares, passing the secret recipe from generation to generation. I kept a small stock only for parties or special occasions—and some specific spells.

The metal spoon clicked against the side of the glass while I stirred the ingredients together.

She watched my motion, her drifting eyes entrapped on the liquid.

"They say he killed Professor Ironhand and then went back for Professor Magnolia."

The boards around me creaked, as though Brew leaned closer to catch her next words too.

"Why would he kill Irabel?" Magnolia makes sense, since intimate partners were more likely to kill each other than any other relationship.

"The Board of Professional Standards," she whispered and wiggled her eyebrows like I should know what that meant too.

And this time, I did.

"He wanted to be on the Board?" I dumped the mixture into her mug and stuck in a fresh stick of rosemary. I passed the drink over the sash slowly, waiting for her next words.

"I—"

Suzie grabbed her friend's arm. "You got your drink." Her voice sounded hard as she shot me a look. "Let's go."

She pulled the others away, disappearing into the shadows as the glowing lanterns replaced the set sun. I tapped my fingers along the sash. I needed to talk to Dominic, and even though it wasn't the best location, now was better than never. Irabel was missing, Magnolia was dead, Perthum refused to cooperate, and I didn't have a single lead.

I pulled off my linen apron and set it over the edge of the inset copper basin. I grabbed a little sign reading '*Be Back Soon!*' and pulled open Brew's back door.

The wagon grumbled.

"I'll be right back." I patted the wooden frame absentmindedly. "I need to talk to someone."

The wood shook against me. I paused. Brew didn't usually complain so much.

"I know I'm not supposed to be working on the case tonight, but it'll be quick. Maybe he'll give me a clothing sample to take to Leof, and he can do a scent map to compare it to the hairs from the murder scene. It'll be two minutes."

Brew groaned again.

I frowned but pulled my hand from the wagon and headed to where Dominic sipped his delicate wine and laughed from deep in his gut, like his long-time partner wasn't killed, and he didn't have a care in the world.

I made it three steps before the night screamed and the ground tore apart.

Chapter 13

The quaking earth threw me against Brew. The wagon shook against my back in a very *I told you so* manner. It had tried to warn me, and even when a sliver of darkness spread across the ground and billows of black smoke covered the courtyard, Brew had a sense of humor.

"Not the right time, Brew," I said.

The wagon's door creaked open with the rumbles of the shaking, affording me a quick peek of Bubbles' startled expression. The warplog spared me a hurried glance, just long enough to thump one back foot in displeasure before hopping out of sight into his cupboard.

Just me, then, to do the whole 'saving the day' thing alone. Again.

The earth stilled. Smoke clustered amongst the courtyard, twisting and turning into two very solid canine shapes. Shadow-Beasts, fresh from whatever pits of hell magic called them from.

My stomach tightened where the claw marks had freshly healed—as though remembering the pain these creatures could inflict.

Heated green embers peered from where their eyes should be.

The glistening color promised blood and terror. They swept their gaze over the crowd, ignoring screams of panic as most party-goers fled in the opposite direction.

Those emerald flames landed on me. The pair locked their gaze, and I stepped away from the wagon. If they attacked, I'd make sure Brew and Bubbles stayed out of danger.

But the Shadow-Beasts barely lingered on me before sweeping back through the crowd. I titled my head, heart racing in my throat, competing with the bud of curiosity sprouting alongside it.

What were they looking for?

One of the beasts bent its front legs, slipping into a hunting position. The lips across its haired nose rose to expose two lines of razor teeth. Its partner followed the line of sight—and saw whatever target they'd found.

The pair moved forward together, into the crowd, wisps of smoke billowing from their hides with each crouching step.

I followed, instincts screaming at me to run the other way. But I couldn't. I remembered the touch of heat and pain from their claws. I needed to prevent that from happening to anyone else.

People parted before me. The wave of terrified citizens thickened near the center of the courtyard, where clusters of wooden tables cradled abandoned plates of food. The beasts headed toward the rear area, where a handful of people cowered beneath the depths of the tables. A sort of smugness lit at the sight of Dominic—moments ago looking so arrogant and cocky with his expensive beverage—huddled beneath the bench, hoping the shadows didn't search for him tonight.

But one person did not cower.

Suzie stood before a toppled cart, where her two friends

crouched and whimpered in fear. The beasts studied her, an intelligence burning in their gaze.

They'd stopped their hunt. Suzie wasn't standing between them and their target—she *was* their target.

Adrenaline laced through my veins. My magic stretched up, the threat of death drawing it near to the surface. I tried to stuff it all down. If I used too much of my power and the King of Erline found me in Hallow's Promise, far, far worse would happen to Suzie and anyone who'd ever known me.

But I refused to let her die. I couldn't fault her for hating me. Being my friend had almost gotten her father killed. But friends protected important people in their lives. I didn't have enough of those to let one die now.

My side burned as I sprinted across the courtyard. Tyfin made me do terrible sprints with heavy weights strapped to my back during some of our swordsmanship lessons. He claimed it was endurance training, but I thought he gained some kind of sick pleasure at my suffering.

I'd never been happier to have trained before.

The first Shadow-Beast leapt as I finished my dash. I ground my teeth and thrust a wall of magic between Suzie and the creature. The wall crumpled with the first contact since I couldn't use enough magic to sustain it. But the beast fell to the ground.

I halted in front of Suzie.

Her hands were glowing.

"Rae," she hissed between her teeth. "You're in my way."

"I—" What?

A stream of light whirled by my ear. I ducked a moment before the second one flew toward the Shadow-Beast. The bulb hit it straight in the chest, and the creature staggered, shook its head, and a soft whimper escaping its lips.

The second one bared its teeth.

Suzie launched two more glowing orbs at it. Only one contacted the beast's front paw, and it dashed away to lick its wounds.

"Wow," I said, the most intelligent thing I could think of. "I didn't know you could do that."

Suzie rolled her eyes. "You don't know me, Rae."

"How many more can you make?"

She spread her fingers. The buzz of magic swirled at the center of her palm, preparing to form into one of those balls again. "Um, maybe three or four?"

"Oh." I couldn't hide the disappointment in my voice.

Suzie crossed her arms. "I'm still learning, okay?"

It wasn't the right time for this discussion. I wanted to tell her that her abilities impressed me, and her demeanor under conflict. But the two beasts had shaken off the lingering effects of the orbs and hunched down to charge us again.

Suzie's hands lit up.

I could build another wall, but I doubted knocking them to the ground over and over would end this fight. Suzie would exhaust her powers before we took even one of them down.

"Brew!" I shouted. A loud groan echoed across the way—Brew letting me know it heard me. "Throw me the vinegar, Salt of Hartshorn, and the booze!"

The wagon groaned. Glasses clinked as Brew pulled the ingredients from the shelves. The first bottle—a corked container of Salt of Hartshorn—flew across the yard. I caught it on the tips of my fingers.

The Shadow-Beasts had paused to watch, a sort of surprised look frozen on their faces. They shook their hides as the second bottle barreled toward me, a streak of glass and vinegar launching through the air.

The booze didn't come.

"Brew! The booze!"

One beast laughed with a howl. Suzie blasted it in the mouth with a glowing ball, but the second beast swiped at her hand before she could launch another attack.

She screamed and backstepped.

"Brew!"

The groans from the wagon grew louder. It shuttered for a moment, then launched a small, golden bottle at me.

I caught it, at the cost of pounding my knees into the hard ground.

Qawha beans.

Their earthy coloring clung to the side of the glass and stained it an amber yellow. The beans grew in warmer climates halfway around the world. I'd tried several blends for it in my drinks, but the bitter taste didn't quite brew joy in the residents of Hallow's Promise.

"What am I supposed to do with this?" I asked, far too quietly for the wagon to hear me.

The Shadow-Beasts crouched again. Suzie's orb spun over my head.

Hopefully Brew knew what it was doing, because all our lives depended on the jar it had just thrown me.

I pulled the corks from all the bottles. A sharp rush of vinegar neutralized with the lighter smell of the Qawha beans. I dumped the entire jar of Salt of Hartshorn into the vinegar.

Bubbles climbed inside of the container immediately. It spilt over the sides and onto the ground—but not enough. I needed to flood the liquid enough for the creatures to step into it.

I studied the beans. They contained the right amount of acidity to boost the bubbling concoction. I'd planned to use the booze to infuse stronger magic, but that would be useless if the beasts never got their paws wet.

Brew knew that. I should have never doubted the wagon.

I raised the small jar to my lips and threw my head back. The beans needed to be ground to expose the interior to the reaction. Without a mortar and pestle, chewing them was the next best option.

The hard beans pressed against my teeth. I sucked in deep breaths through my nose, trying not to choke as far too many filled my mouth.

Suzie launched an orb over my head. She thrust her fist out for another shot, but the light flickering in the center of her palm dimmed out.

She pulled her hand back and studied it for a moment, like her brain couldn't quite comprehend the sudden dimness. Then, she wiped her hand on her breeches and looked at me, where I knelt and chewed with ferocity.

"If you're going to do something, Rae, now's your chance. Maybe you're only one."

I spit the beans into the bubbling mixture.

Chapter 14

The reaction exploded on contact with the ground beans. The liquid turned the bubbles a dirty brown color, but the concoction seeped into a thick layer across the ground. It lapped at the Shadow-Beasts' paws. They tilted their heads, observing the fluid with an intense gaze.

I thrust my hands into the liquid. My magic coiled around, thick and heavy. I tugged at one careful strand. Simple magic blended into the ebb and flow of regular power. Using anything stronger or specific to my necromantic magic would light me like a beacon for the king to find.

The creatures realized Suzie's powers had faded. One charged again.

I pressed the magic into the potion. It snapped in a dangerous arc from the center of my body, through my hands, and into the fluid. Electric pulses flung across the wet ground, licking against anything touching it.

The beast realized its mistake with the first jolt of magic lightning that lapped at its wet paw. It yelped, a high pitched, terrible sound that made the hairs on the back of my neck stand up. The creature turned, attempting to flee, but I released another swift hit of magic. Silver sparks flew as the lightning flowed into the creature's body.

The current trapped its muscles and froze it into the liquid. As the creature squirmed, more power whipped into it. Piece-by-piece, the Shadow-Beast faded into black smoke, eaten away by my magic, until nothing except ash lingered on the ground.

I let out a sigh. One down—one to go.

"Rae!" Suzie screamed.

I spun around. The second beast had circled behind us. It squinted at me, almost a dare to try my lightning magic again. It stood on a raised half-wall beyond the reach of my potion, its paws now dry.

Its glowing gaze whipped back to Suzie.

She ran.

The Shadow-Beast gave chase, and I cursed in my mind. My legs shook as I forced them to stand. All my plans had ended with the potion and my lightning.

The creature jumped. Its claws dug into Suzie's back, a victorious yelp emitting from its twisted maw.

The world narrowed. All the doubt and panic slipped from my mind. My training with Tyfin sharpened in a moment. I saw the steps I needed to take, where my weight would shift, and I longed to feel my blade cut through the beast's neck.

"Brew," I said. My voice was light. It shouldn't have been audible, but the part of my soul that connected with the sentient wagon knew Brew heard me. "My sword."

The sheathed sword spiraled overhead, launched through the open sash. Seconds slowed as I reached up and plucked the weapon from the air. I drew the blade in the next motion, dropping the leather sheath to the ground.

The Shadow-Beast lifted a sharpened claw over Suzie's quivering back. Darkness pushed away the rest of the world as I raced toward them. Only Suzie, my blade, and my target remained.

Those piercing claws rained down.

My blade was faster.

Hot blood spilled across my hands as my sword impacted the creature's neck. It didn't make a sound as its head tumbled to the side, its body to the other.

I let out my breath, holding my stance. The creature evaporated into smoke and dust.

Color returned to my vision. I fell to my knees and turned Suzie over, afraid to find that I'd been too late, afraid the worst had already happened.

Her eyes flicked open. "Rae," she whispered. My heartbeat again, a pain of relief cutting through me. "That was pretty badass."

I laughed, fear and adrenaline and disbelief swirling together. I smoothed a few strands of hair from Suzie's sweaty forehead. "I'm sorry I didn't get here soon enough. We need to go to my house so I can tend the wound on your back before it turns your insides to ash."

"Before it does . . . what?"

"Don't worry, I won't let that happen." I put my arms around her and helped her up. She grimaced and shook in my grasp, but didn't complain.

We slowly walked toward Brew, one staggering step at a time.

"Where did you learn to do that?" Suzie asked.

I shrugged. "My upbringing was very limited, so when I came to Hallow's Promise, I decided to learn everything I could. I basically lived in the library for my first year here. Any books on basic magic, healing, teas, and tonics, I read everything, and I practiced. Eventually, I realized how my magic could help other people, and I found Brew, and now I'm here fighting Shadow-Beasts."

She gave a small laugh. "But you taught yourself all of that?"

"It didn't feel like I had a choice. If I wanted to stop being powerless, I needed to find ways to strengthen myself."

Suzie looked at me, really looked at me. A sort of gleam filled her eyes, the same glowing yellow that created a ball of liquid light in her palms.

"Can you teach me?"

I almost stumbled. "I—I thought you hated me."

She rolled her eyes. "I'm allowed to change my mind." Her voice softened. "Besides, I don't think I'm allowed to hate someone that risked their life to save mine. You didn't have to do that, but you did."

My cheeks heated. Words swirled in my thoughts, but I couldn't bring them to my lips.

We reached Brew, and the door swung open at our approach. I helped Suzie step inside and closed the door behind us. Her face looked a little green, and I knew from recent experience how much the wounds hurt.

"Suzie," I said as Brew buzzed with magic, preparing to take us home. "I'd love to teach you everything I can."

The world twisted and tilted as Brew found a ley-line and pointed us toward home, but I saw Suzie smile around barred teeth.

Chapter 15

Valen leaned against my front door with his arms crossed and that stupid smile on his lips. My wards popped softly, warning him that the Lightning-Crotch was prepared to strike should he dare to attempt to cross the threshold. He headed toward us as I navigated Suzie out of the wagon.

"I heard you had another Shadow-Beast encounter." He took up her other arm and slung it over his shoulder. Suzie didn't protest, her skin turning more pale than green. Her breaths came in quick pants. "I brought some more salve."

A million snappy comments pulsed through my mind, but all I said was, "Thank you."

The wards lifted as we walked through my door. Krissa stood from the fireplace hearth, her mouth forming into a circle.

"What happened?"

"Shadow-Beasts, again. They attacked us at the party."

Valen and I set Suzie face down on the couch. I used the existing slashes on her shirt to rip away the rest of the fabric. Twin angry lines cut through her skin, letting thick globs of blood escape down her back. Smoke edged around the perimeter of the wounds.

"Is it bad?" she asked, voice muffled from the cushions.

"Define 'bad,'" Krissa said.

"Stop scaring her," I snapped. "Go get a wet rag from the kitchen and the witch hazel from the cabinet. Suzie, you're going to be fine."

Krissa disappeared into the house and returned a moment later, her arms filled with supplies. She passed them to me.

"They were trying to kill you again?"

I pressed my lips as I applied a generous amount of witch hazel over the cuts. The natural antibiotic would help prevent infection. The Shadow-Beasts *had* seen me—we'd locked gazes across the courtyard, but they'd turned their backs to me. The attack seemed targeted—for Suzie.

I shook my head. "I don't think they wanted me."

Valen handed me a small glass jar. I twisted the top and the familiar scent of herbs and mint slipped through. I pressed some onto my fingers and softly rubbed them across the gashes.

The smoke stopped immediately.

Suzie laying on my couch with blood pooling across her skin drudged up memories from the past. My hands started shaking. I tried to smooth the cream across her back, but tears clouded my vision. It hadn't been very long since Leof laid in a very similar position, bearing very similar wounds. Those injuries had been my fault, and these were too. Suzie surviving the attack was miraculous. How long before I'd bear the weight of another person's death?

Valen put his hand over mine. Warmth soaked into me, and he squeezed my fingers lightly. The pressure reminded me to breathe. The air came in ragged, harsh.

"I can finish this," he said. "You've done good, Sunshine."

I pulled my hand back. Suzie's soft breaths told me she'd relaxed, maybe even enough to doze slightly. I tried to smile at the mercenary, to be nonchalant, but my lips refused to budge. I stumbled to my feet, backing up, going . . . somewhere.

My wards tugged in my mind. Someone entered my property. I headed to the door, and a murmur of multiple voices leaked from the other side. I recognized Leof's warm tone and tugged the door open.

The wolf gaped at me with his fist raised toward the door.

"Don't worry, she's going to be fine," I said.

"I—" He blinked. "What? Who's going to be fine?" He lifted his nose into the air and inhaled deeply. "Is that blood?"

I creased my brow. "Suzie. I brought her here after the Shadow-Beast attack at the party. I cleaned the wounds and applied some healing balm. She'll be sore for a couple of days but . . ."

Leof's face twisted. His usual, composed expression flattened, then turned red, and half-formed words tumbled from his mouth.

"I. What. Who. I—"

I glanced over the marshal's shoulder. Three other constables, including Castor, clustered on the stoop behind Leof. Their stoic expressions made my shoulders tense.

"You didn't know Suzie was here," I stated flatly. "You didn't know about the Shadow-Beast attack."

"We knew about the attack, but not that you were involved, or Suzie." Leof tried to shoulder into the house, but I held my ground. The wolf stilled, his eyes flashing a dangerous shade of gold. "Let me see my daughter."

"Why are you here, Leof?" I let my power soften my voice. The calm before the storm.

"I need to see Suzie."

The fire burning in his gaze far surpassed any of his marshal roles. They were flames that only parents could ignite when their children faced danger or pain.

I stepped aside. I hoped that when the Providers came for me, my parents had the same look in their eyes, the knowledge that they'd fight to the death before surrendering me. Leof had every right to see Suzie.

Castor tried to follow him. I threw my wards up, a shimmering glow between me and him. He froze, a handspan before he touched that dangerous shield.

I crossed my arms and studied the constable on the other side. I let one side of my lips tilt up, a sly smile, a dare for him to cross the wards.

He thrust his hand into a pocket on his vest and removed a slip of parchment. He unfolded it and held it out, allowing me to read the scrawled text through the magic.

By decree of the Office of the Sheriff, as granted per the Capital of Erline, ruled by the King unto Himself, shall the following named be deemed of arrest by the foretold crime:
Krissa Camalany Enver for murder by hire

I blinked. The words remained the same. A coolness spread from the top of my head into the tips of my fingers. My magic coiled inside that ice—the dead in my soul crawling its way out.

"What evidence do you have?" My breath froze inside my throat, and the air came out foggy from the cold.

Castor held up another parchment, this one discolored and worn, with a broken red wax seal holding the two halves together. He opened it, letting me read the page.

A letter—confirming a receipt of payment, signed with

Krissa's name at the bottom.

Castor folded the page. "We found it during the search of her property. It was hidden in a space beneath the floorboards. We've summoned the sheriff for the trial. He'll arrive in three days. It's all legal. She can come out willingly or we can use force."

If they found her guilty at trial, the punishment for murder was death.

Castor would die before he entered my home.

The shimmering shield between us turned a vivid blue, the color of glacier water through a raging river. The Lightning-Crotch became something stronger, something that reeked of death and decay, and made a dark happiness swell inside me. If the man entered through the wards, he would die, and the king would find me within moments.

But threatening to hurt my friend—for that, I may suffer, but Castor would first.

I flicked my fingers at Castor. *Come here, come see what beast you've awoken.*

Softness touched my arm. Where the ice turned my skin white, Krissa's warmth seeped into my flesh. She ran her hand along my skin and gave me a tight smile. She pressed her lips against my ear, the words for me alone. The scent of honeysuckle and blueberries escaped from her hair and clothes.

"Don't do that, Rae. Don't bring the capital here, not yet. Find the real killer, bring them to justice." She squeezed my arm.

Krissa laughed, but through the blue haze over my vision, she squared her shoulders, and clenched her hands. A buzz of anxiety revealed through the sweat from her palm onto my skin. But she smiled, released my arm, and stepped toward the wards.

"Wait." I grabbed her and pulled her into a tight hug. I put my lips to her ear. "I will find the killer, but if I don't, I will kill anyone that puts you to trial."

"It's a promise, then," she said.

Krissa crossed the wards, a warm blast of sunshine against my death-cold magic. Castor lifted chains to her arms. Anger swam through me, my promise to Krissa the only thing keeping the constable alive.

She gave me one last glance as they led her toward a set of horses—light dancing from her rainbow bows, the frills at the edge of her dress darting playfully—and she *smiled*.

All her hope . . . in me.

Another coolness, not so different from the death and darkness of my magic spilling in angry waves through my house, pulsed behind me.

Valen.

He smelled like evergreen and mint, violence and promise.

"Do you want me to kill them?" he asked, as though he knew exactly what my magic wanted to do, but couldn't, not yet.

"No," I said. Our twin angers met and mixed and Suzie's blood stained the air. "But I do need your help."

"Anything, Sunshine."

"What do you know about harloons?"

Valen remained silent for a heartbeat, the harsh rage softening.

"About . . . what?"

Chapter 16

The Central College for Mages and Magic might have been haunted, or it at least looked that way at night. Shadows clung to the stone walls and sent eerie shapes across the ground in the moonlight. Flashes of motion danced at the edge of my vision before darting away when I turned to look. Musty air pushed against my face—moisture and decay like the dead.

"So, we're breaking into a high-ranking mage's office in the middle of the night on a rather creepy college campus to capture a monkey? Did I get that right?"

Valen's form slipped into the shadows like familiar arms welcoming him home. His clothing wasn't even all dark. A worn leather jacket covered the arms of his white tunic, leaving the front exposed, including the top two buttons that he hadn't fastened. I tried to avoid looking below his eyes when we spoke, or I feared he'd catch my wandering gaze.

While the mercenary was all shadow and deception, I felt like a lit torch among the shrubs. I'd donned all black clothing. It didn't matter. Parts of me didn't hug the foliage quite right, leaving one foot and most of the left side of my body exposed. Anyone walking by would slip right past Valen in their pursuit of me.

"It's not a monkey, it's a harloon," I said for the hundredth time.

"I am really not seeing a difference." The mercenary shrugged. I hated that his evergreen and forest scent strengthened when he did that—and not because it made my heartbeat arrhythmically. "How is catching the harpoon going to help get Krissa out of prison?"

"*Harloon*. We found hairs on the victim's body at the crime scene. Leof scent mapped them, and if that map matches the harloon, that makes Perthum a suspect."

"Why would Perthum want to kill his own employee?"

I ground my teeth. "Who knows? Sometimes the motive isn't clear to anyone except the killer."

Valen studied me. He tipped one side of his mouth into a half smile. "Alright, Sunshine, let's go get your harryspoon hair sample."

He moved across the campus before I corrected him again. I sucked in a deep breath and held it until my lungs complained and let it out slowly. One murder had already occurred on this campus. I didn't need to cause a second one.

Our strip of hedges rested on the outer perimeter of the main campus entryway. According to Valen, it was ironically the less protected entrance since campus security didn't expect troublemakers to use the front door. A sprawling expanse of green grass crept between us and the archway curving around the entrance.

The cold danced over my skin, and I rubbed my arms. The sooner we got the harloon's hair sample, the sooner I could leave and only return during daytime hours with Brew.

I couldn't see the mercenary as I veered into the openness—hopefully in his footsteps. The grass gave beneath my feet, cushioning every step. Soft light from a guard's torch crossed over the walkway on the far right of the field, but its golden rays never touched me.

The lit archway grew closer, and a flash of a shadow darted toward the door. I froze, anticipating the growl and lunge of another Shadow-Beast, but it was Valen, already propping the door open.

I knelt beside him, chest heaving with deep breaths from the run and worry of being caught. The college was one of the best places for me to sell teas and tonics. If the dean revoked my selling rights, I'd be in major financial trouble. Being a Crime Investigation Expert didn't begin to cover all my expenses.

Valen slipped the door open and gestured for me to enter.

"Ladies first," he said.

"Then lead the way," I snapped.

He chuckled, but stepped into the hall. He waited until I entered before closing the wooden door.

A long hallway slipped in either direction. Rows of doors lined both ways, each leading to a different type of lecture hall or office. I headed to the left, where Leof and I had visited Perthum's office last time.

We moved carefully, slowly. Students could come and go from the dormitory wing on the opposite side of campus, but all lecture halls were closed at sunset. If anyone saw us, we'd have a lot of questions to answer.

"How much farther?" Valen whispered.

"We're almost—"

Valen half growled, half grunted. He grabbed my arm with one hand and threw open the closest door with the other. He pulled me inside and shut the door with barely a click.

"What—"

He put his hand over my mouth. "Shhh."

I opened my mouth to bite the man's palm—right in the tender spot beneath the thumb where sensitive nerves ran close to the skin—when I heard it: footsteps from the hall.

The mercenary raised his brows and smiled.

He'd thrown us into some type of closet, barely enough room for both of us to stand facing each other. Brooms and jugs of liquid stacked on the other side. It smelled like bleach, dust, mist, and pine.

The last scents came from Valen's hand, still touching my mouth. I looked up to his face—intending to tell him off, I promise—but he already stared at me. The words caught in my throat. A blush worked its way up my cheeks at the intensity of his gaze on my face.

Valen moved his hand to the side of my jaw and brushed this thumb across the space beneath my lower lip. Chills sprung along my skin as warmth climbed up the center of my body. I raised my chin, or maybe it raised itself, but I wanted that rich sensation to grow, and I knew putting my lips on Valen's would build it into a rich, bursting fire.

He sucked in a gasp. His icy blue eyes twirled with their own flames. He leaned closer.

I thought he would kiss me. I considered closing my eyes, but I wanted to see that desire, craved the attention promised to me. His ice and fire overwhelmed me, spreading the tingles from my lips to my chest and lower.

Valen leaned his forehead against mine. I tensed, the action unexpected. He breathed heavily, as though I was the only oxygen remaining in the room.

The tension and flutters slowly stilled. I took in a deep, shuddering breath, and Valen did too. I closed my eyes.

We stayed that way for more than a few heartbeats. Two people, alone in a world riddled with violence and chaos, trying desperately to make some sort of difference in our own ways.

Valen pulled away. The footsteps had long since faded.

He opened the door, letting a chilled air inside, far cooler than I remembered it being. My body complained at his absence and the sudden space between us. I told it to be quiet. Kissing Valen would have been a mistake. He didn't have commitments and he didn't stick around. Thank goodness he'd had enough sense to stop the situation.

He hesitated in the doorway. "You'll be the death of me, Sunshine."

* * *

Dean Perthum's office was dark. Valen snatched a single, used candle from the dean's desk and struck a match with one hand. The soft glow illuminated enough to see, but not well.

"How do you know he doesn't take the harlot home with him every night?" Valen ran his hand along the oak desk, his brows raised in a sort of appreciation expression.

"The *harloon* had its own room. I'm guessing it's a permanent residence."

"Guessing?" Valen shook his head. "I should have known you were making this up as you went."

I ground my teeth and rounded the desk toward the door on the other side. He wasn't completely wrong. I didn't have real training as a Crime Investigation Expert—only some knowledge and a lot of stubbornness.

I rattled the knob. "It's locked."

"Move over." Valen knelt at the lock. His wide shoulders blocked my view, but a mechanical jingle emitted every couple of seconds. The seams of his jacket tightened when he flexed—not that I watched him flex, it just happened. A moment later, the lock tumbled and clicked open.

"How'd you do that?" I leaned closer, studying the lock for signs of damage. "Was it magic?"

"No magic necessary. A person in my . . . career field needs to know how to open a few locked doors."

"Would you show me?" I asked, a sort of awe overshadowing any kind of sense.

He winked at me. "I'll show you anything you ask for, Sunshine."

I blushed again at the implication of his words, but he pushed the door open and cast the subtle light into the room.

Twin brown eyes blinked at us, reflecting the light back from their very center. The harloon crawled out of a fabric shelter on a raised platform.

I hadn't caught a great look at it during the first visit to Perthum's office. It did most closely resemble the cross between a cat and a monkey, but that wasn't quite right. Its snout pushed into its face, so the nostrils barely peeked from the thick gray fur. The front limbs stretched disproportionately long, almost as long as the curling tail at its rear. The creature opened its furry mouth and released a high-pitched, chattery greeting.

Valen flinched. "You want a fur sample from *that*?"

"Yep."

"Of course you do."

The mercenary smiled and tried to lower his voice to a more

soothing pitch. "Hi there." He crept forward. "We just need to borrow a little bit of fur, and then we'll be on our way. We'd barely interrupt your beauty sleep."

The harloon tilted its head and curiously watched the man's slow approach.

"It seems friendly," I said.

"So does a Spike-Shroom, until you step on one."

I couldn't argue with that. They closely resembled dark mushrooms, but hid a long, hard spear inside their fleshy exterior. I hadn't stepped on one myself—yet.

Valen reached the edge of the platform. The harloon looked directly down at him.

"He's wearing a collar with a tag," Valen said.

"What's it say?"

"Dutchess Frideswide."

"It does not."

"Yes, it does. Here, I'll show you." Valen reached toward the animal. A sparkle flashed in—apparently *her*—eyes.

I recognized the look as pure trouble. "Valen . . ."

Dutchess gleefully sailed over Valen's outstretched arms. He watched her arc with wide eyes, tracking where she would land, moments too late.

She plopped on top of his head and shrieked. Valen screamed too, almost matching Dutchess' tone. He flung his arms up, trying to grab her, but she spun in circles, expertly avoiding his touch, except for when she flicked her tail into his face.

A laugh boiled at the bottom of my gut. The man—a known killer, a paid mercenary, darkness and shadows personified—danced around the room, releasing the occasional yell and grunt while waving his arms as an attempt to pluck the harloon from his head.

I tried to hold it back, I really did, but that laugh pushed up and up until it slipped out of my mouth and into the chaos of the room. The dam broke, releasing my laughter along with Valen's shouts. I laughed until a stitch pinched my side and I wheezed for air.

Dutchess seemed to notice my sound after a moment. She paused her frantic pulling of Valen's hair to look at me.

That sparkle returned.

I backpedaled, both hands held out, pleading. "No, no, no."

She leapt.

I screamed.

Her little hands clawed into my longer hair, pulling it from the ties I'd bound it with. I shrieked too and heard Valen laughing from across the room as I twisted and circled and tried to grab Dutchess. Her soft fur slipped out of my grasp.

She chuckled, enjoying herself far too much.

Another yell intertwined with our screams and her laughs—from outside.

Valen stopped laughing. His face turned serious from one moment to the next.

"The guards are coming," he said. "We're out of time."

I tried again to grab the animal, but she ducked under my hands to crawl down my back. "No! I have to get the sample for Leof to compare it!" Or Krissa would go to trial, and I may have to kill a whole lot of people to save her life.

"Fine. I didn't want to do this, but . . ."

Silence spanned for a handful of seconds. Then an icy chill swept over us. Dutchess paused, two fistfuls of my hair in her tiny fingers.

I stopped too. Where Valen had been, a dark stranger stood. Shadows fell from his skin, softening his form into the dark.

Gone was the evergreen and forest, replaced with the scent of violence and a craving for blood.

"What are you waiting for?" The Lord of Dark asked. "Grab the buffoon's hair and let's go!"

Oh, right.

I snatched the shocked animal and grabbed a cluster of hair near the roots. "Sorry, Dutchess," I said as I pulled.

She didn't do more than scratch at the space where the fur came loose in my hand. She kept her eyes on whatever Valen was, a buried instinct warning her this predator liked to play chase.

"I got it!" I thrust my hand up, gray hair raining over me.

The voices grew louder. I glanced toward the door, half expecting it to open to a group of guards. When I looked back, Valen was Valen again.

He grabbed my other hand and took us into the hallway.

Shadows danced on the wall from the far end as the guards neared. Once they rounded the corner, they'd see us.

He shut the door, trapping Dutchess inside. Perthum would realize someone had been in his office as soon as he arrived in the morning. Our attempts to catch the harloon sort of rearranged all the papers, books, and cushions.

"Run," Valen whispered. "This way."

He pulled me, and we ran.

Chapter 17

The night air kissed us as we emerged from the college. We'd crossed through two different wings of the campus before Valen decided it was safe to exit. Sweat coated my palms, and I hoped my scent didn't overwhelm that of the fur in my hand.

Valen slowed as we moved across the grass, dropping his grip from my hand in the process. I should have been happy when the coolness brushed against my skin, but a small part of me mourned the loss of contact.

A flood of relief spilled from my shoulders down the rest of my body. We'd done it. We'd gotten a hair sample from the harloon to compare to the evidence from Magnolia's body. If these matched, I'd have plenty of proof placing Dean Parthum as the killer and freeing Krissa from the ridiculous allegations.

I smiled.

"Hey!" The sound rang across campus.

I froze, and Valen tensed beside me. His hand slipped to his waist, where I knew some sort of weapon resided.

I pivoted, expecting to see the guards we'd evaded to have caught up. Instead, a somewhat familiar-shaped person jogged across the grass, with black robes billowing in their wake.

"We should go," Valen whispered.

"Hold on." I squinted into the dark. "I might know them."

The man slowed as he approached, his breathing a bit ragged. His dark hair blended into the night, and a short, tidy goatee perched at the bottom of his face. Professor Dominic wore an emerald green vest tonight, similar in shape to the maroon one he'd worn previously at the party in the Shrine District. A silver handkerchief sat in the upper pocket, flashing in the moonlight.

"You're—" He caught his breath. "You're the lady from the party. The one that killed those terrible creatures that attacked us!"

"Um, yeah, I guess that is me." I scratched at the back of my neck awkwardly.

Dominic straightened. "It was amazing." He gestured wildly with his hands, reenacting the events with imaginary weapons and magic. "First, you went, 'Give me the magic potion.' Then, they just appeared, and BAM, lightning everywhere. Next, you were all, 'Don't hurt my friend.' And suddenly you had a sword, and woah, and then they were gone! Impressive, very impressive."

Valen raised a brow at me. "Impressive, indeed," he said.

"Well, thank you. It was, uh, the least I could do." Especially since the alternative was watching them kill Suzie, then probably me.

"After all that, though, I didn't expect to see you again, nonetheless, on my campus in the middle of the night. I haven't even gotten your name."

"Rae," I said, sort of stiffly. I had questions for the professor, but his openness and enthusiasm caught me by surprise.

"Rae," he repeated, a sort of wonder in his tone. "Rae, that's lovely, just lovely. Listen, if you would be at all interested, I'd love to take you to dinner one night this week. My treat, of course. I want to hear you recount the story all over again. Perhaps I can write it down. It would be a wonderful treat for my students to learn from. Shall we call it a date, maybe?"

He waited with wide, hopeful eyes while I tried to find words, any words to respond.

Valen straightened beside me. That coolness swirled around us, the edges of his power spurned from anger.

Was he *jealous* that Dominic just asked to court me?

My voice refused to respond to the demands in my mind. I sort of gaped my mouth open and shut, waiting for something, anything, to happen.

"Magnolia," I finally choked out.

"Ah," Dominic nodded, apparently unsurprised that I spit out his deceased partner's name in response to his request for a date. "Yes, you must have heard that we used to be together. Her loss is a tragedy, to this college and society as a whole, as well as myself. She was a bit quirky, but a genius, actually. She had big plans for this town and served rigorously on the Board of Professional standards. In fact, Magnolia learned days before her death that she'd been chosen for the coveted wish—though I believe she died before it could be fulfilled. He shook his head. "Such a shame."

I tried to sift through all the information he'd spilled out in a few heartbeats. Nobody else had described Magnolia's personality as 'quirky,' more like cutthroat and rude.

And her wish would have been granted. Even Dean Parthum hadn't seemed to know that.

"Do you know what her wish would have been?"

"Oh, yes. She longed for a way to heal any ailment. She almost had a child once, you see, but it became ill before birth and entered this world asleep. Magnolia wanted to spare others that pain. She longed for some kind of universal healing."

"*Magnolia* almost had a child?" Valen asked, his tone a mix of that frozen anger and reluctant curiosity. I had the same question, but was too polite to ask. Magnolia didn't sound like she had been the maternal type.

Dominic nodded. "Oh, yes, well before we ever met. I'm sure it's not possible to recover from a wound like that, not all the way, at least. If anyone could defeat death, it would have been Magnolia. She wanted to help people, and Hallow's Promise could reap any financial benefits by becoming a centralized location for healing. Lots of visitors would boost the town's economy. She always thought about the whole picture."

"Doesn't the college have a Magical Healing department?"

He snorted. "Yes, one of the best, as Perthum likes to say. But current magical healing is so fickle. Magnolia wanted something more stable."

I bit my lip. I vaguely recalled that Professor Irabel Ironhand had taught Introduction to Magical Healing. Could it be a coincidence that she went missing as Magnolia tried to improve the healing field as well? Maybe a motive to her murder revolved around someone attempting to stop the progression of the medical field.

"You must be familiar with my relationship with Magnolia, since you've asked so much about her." Dominic continued. "I did love Magnolia once, long ago. She made it very apparent that her work and ambition will come before me, always. I . . . I couldn't live like that. That's not a partnership. It's not real love. We've been apart for several years, nothing more than friends. I still care deeply about her, of course. I even took in her beloved cat after she passed. Sure, it ran away immediately, but I did try." Dominic subtly wiped a tear from his eye.

"Thank you for—wait, did you say cat?" I clutched the fur in my hand.

"Oh, yes. Whiskers, she called him. He was quite a new adoption, actually. Very long hair, very affectionate. He was rather pleasant for the few days I had him."

"What color is Whiskers?" I asked, even as my heart sank. Any hair on Magnolia's body likely came from that cat, and not the suspect, after all.

"He's a bit of a mix, but mostly gray and black. His front feet are all white. Very cute, very cute, indeed."

Dominic continued on as though he hadn't crushed my world. All my work hinged on those hairs coming from the murderer. Breaking into Perthum's office and stealing the fur from the harloon—useless.

Valen put his hand on my shoulder. I sucked in a breath.

They had Krissa trapped in prison. She was relying on me, and all I had was a magic cast and an unreliable expert to try to decipher it.

I would have to visit Fraya tomorrow. We'd have two days before the Sheriff arrived. I'd *make* the woman give me some answers about the magic cast this time.

"What do you say, Rae?" Dominic asked, a lighter tone in his voice. "Can I take you out to dinner? It would be such a pleasure."

The opportunity to annoy Valen basically stared me in the face, but I couldn't muster the energy. I had almost nothing to clear Krissa's name. Dutchess had taken more of my hair than I'd gotten from her. I'd been up all night and Suzie still rested at my house, wounded and tired.

I wanted to go to bed.

"Sorry, Dominic. I'm not really looking for a relationship right now." No, I was looking for a murderer and failing miserably.

The professor caught my hand—the one without a damp wad of fur—and pressed my knuckles to his lips. "Next time, then. You know where to find me." He winked, ducked his head to Valen, and set off.

I sighed.

"The fur is still valuable," Valen said. That anger had disappeared as rapidly as ice in the first brush of spring. "Leof can eliminate Perthum, at least."

"Yeah." I twisted the strands in my fingers. The gray color matched my mood. "Let's go home."

Chapter 18

My knife smacked against the cutting board. The countertop shook. Glass bottles of oils, potion bases, and various syrups pulsed with each slice of the blade into the lemons.

Leof, Suzie, and Valen sat near the kitchen, each watching me from the corner of their eyes. Leof flinched every time the knife hammered down. Bubbles blinked at the noise from his perch in Suzie's lap. He didn't offer any eyeball licks this time.

Smack, smack, smack.

"So, it didn't go well?" the wolf finally asked.

I grabbed the next lemon and slashed the knife through it.

Smack.

"The mission was successful," Valen answered the marshal, though he carefully averted his gaze from the wolf and me. "But it may have been futile."

"You did get the fur, though?"

Anger colored the pale lemons a vivid red. I clenched the knife handle tighter in my fist. I'd chosen a simple paring knife, but wished it was the butcher's blade at the top of the rack.

"It. Doesn't. Matter." I bit out the words, slicing blindly into the fruit. It fell into pieces that rolled around the surface of the cutting board before finally falling onto their sides. I studied the chopped citrus. A white core perched in the center and the lobes of juice expanded outward. They'd been crushed, expelling acidic liquid all over my countertop.

I felt like that lemon. I'd done everything right. Becoming Hallow's Promise's Crime Investigation Expert was supposed to put my quirky knowledge to good use. Having Krissa as a friend made my life—and hopefully hers—richer.

And it didn't matter.

I sucked in a deep breath. My chest quivered at the very top of the inhale.

Leof stood and rounded the counter into the kitchen. He gently touched my hand until my fingers uncurled and the knife fell. The werewolf gathered me into his arms. He locked me in a tight hug, one I didn't know I'd needed.

My breath came out in a sob. Hot tears spilled down my cheeks and a harsh gulp escaped through my lips. My vision blurred, no longer red with rage. Tears soaked into Leof's shirt, but he didn't recoil from the dampness. He held me longer and I welcomed the solid warmth.

A moment later, another, smaller set of arms encircled us. Suzie stood beside her father, wrapping me in a similar embrace. She smelled like sugar and smoke.

Valen's chair scratched along the ground, but he didn't join us. He stood to the side, a sort of blank expression on his face. When he caught my stare, he gave me a smile and a wink, which I knew was the most he could give right now.

"Did you expect friendship to be easy, Rae?" Leof asked softly.

I gulped again. "I didn't expect to worry about someone I cared for so much—ever."

"Worrying is hard. The fear is worse. But having a true

friend by your side is worth all the pain and heartache that comes along with them. You're putting your heart and soul into getting Krissa out of prison. She knows that. She trusts you."

"What if I can't do it?" I whispered. Silence settled around us for a moment.

"You can," Suzie answered.

"You will," Valen said, almost at the same time.

A quiet spread through the kitchen and twisted around the rest of the house. I'd lived in silence in the capital for years and years—cold and dark and hopeless. This kind of silence was different. There was color between the beats of our hearts. Leof and Suzie's soft breathing against me drew a calmness from the depths of my soul that I'd never felt before.

If I had the ability to stop time, this moment would tempt me more than almost any other.

But I didn't, and Krissa was counting on me—on us.

I pulled back slightly, and Leof and Suzie loosened their grips. They stepped away while I wiped the tears from my eyes, but they lingered.

"I'm okay," I whispered. "Thank you."

Leof squeezed my shoulder before guiding Suzie back to their seats, but Valen stayed by the kitchen, close to me.

I returned to my lemons and laughed at the carnage waiting for me. "You just stood there and watched me butcher these poor lemons?"

Suzie grimaced. "We were too afraid to say anything."

Bubbles, back to his place in her lap, licked one eyeball in agreement.

The next lemon perched in the center of the cutting board, and I carefully slipped the small knife into its thick skin. It split evenly, right down the center, hardly any juice wasted from the cut.

Much better.

"We got the fur sample from Dutchess," I said.

"Dutchess?" Leof raised his brows.

"The typhoon," Valen answered.

"The *harloon*. We got the fur sample, but we met with Professor Dominic, Magnolia's previous partner, on our way off campus. He told us Magnolia had a cat."

"Oh, no."

"A gray cat," I stated.

Leof muttered under his breath, "Damn it."

I nodded. "I know. But you should check the sample anyway, just to make sure it really came from Magnolia's cat and that Perthum isn't involved. I'm talking to Fraya tomorrow about the magic cast. It's the best evidence we have right now."

"Alivia might have more information about the body." Leof laughed when he caught sight of my face. "I know she's not your favorite person, but she's damn good at what she does."

I set the first half of the lemon into the juice press and squeezed the handle. Rich, sharp liquid slipped into the glass beneath the press. I tossed the peel into the compost bin and snatched the next half.

"Fine. I will go talk to Alivia, but I won't be happy about it."

"You could also visit Krissa," Leof said.

I missed the glass, and more juice poured over my countertop. My heart jumped. "I can visit her?"

"Sure." Leof shrugged. "Visiting hours are from noontime to sunset."

A thin bubble of happiness inflated in my chest. I could visit Krissa and make sure she was alright.

"Thank you for telling me that, Leof. I'll see Krissa tomorrow." I barely believed that to be the truth. "Could you grab the cauldron from the fire?"

I asked Leof, but it was Valen who moved toward the flames. He fished the boiling water, cardamom, and anise concoction from the heat and rested it on the pad beside me.

"Thanks," I said.

"Anytime, Sunshine." He spoke low enough for the words to float between us. I swallowed a sudden lump in my throat.

I set out four mugs and spooned an equal amount of the mixture into each. Admittedly, I may have added an extra few sips into my cup. Next, I blended a healthy amount of fresh honey bought from my neighbors, a few spoonfuls of the squeezed citrus juice, and topped them with those stupid, round slices of lemon at the edge of the rims.

The fruit and honey blended together, a slight sweet against the more herby flavors of the cardamom and anise. Even though it wasn't cold outside, the heat of the mug in my hand settled an ache deep in my gut.

Everyone sighed at the first sip.

"I'm going to scent map this fur and compare it to the evidence from the body," Leof said.

"And I will talk to Fraya and Alivia, then visit Krissa at the prison," I replied.

"I'm going with you," Suzie demanded.

A choking sound came from Leof's direction.

Suzie crossed her arms and sent her dad a glare. "You can't stop me."

He half-nodded, half shook his head. "I know." He looked at me. "It's up to her."

I bit my lip. On one hand, I didn't want to risk putting

Suzie in danger, but on the other, she'd launched several high-powered light balls at two Shadow-Beasts less than ten hours ago. She'd asked me to train her. If that's what she really wanted, it was a good idea for her to come with me.

"That's fine," I said. "But our first stop has to be the butcher's shop."

"Why?"

I glanced at the warplog on her lap, who may have been eyeing Suzie's hand with just a hint of acid drool seeping from the corner of his mouth.

"No particular reason," I said.

Chapter 19

The butcher's store sat at the end of downtown. It was far enough to the edge that visitors didn't usually wander in accidentally, but close enough for locals to stop by for some fresh meat while completing their regular errands. A little bell jingled over the door when we stepped inside moments before sunrise, happily running on about four hours of sleep. Tired? Who's tired? Can't be me.

A man with a blood-stained apron stood behind the counter. He fixed his spectacles as we walked in and sighed a lukewarm sound.

"Welcome, Rae. Welcome, Bubbles. Let me fetch Matilda—she'll wring my neck if she misses you."

Gerome, Matilda's husband, disappeared behind the simple sheet that separated the customers from the rest of the shop. A moment later, a squat woman entered from the same sheet. Her dark hair coiled into a bun at the nape of her neck, and the usual giant knife Matilda carried was nowhere to be seen.

"Oh, just look at you." She circled the counter toward us, arms stretched open. Suzie, hardly half a step behind my heels, recoiled as though expecting the woman to embrace her. But Matilda bent to scoop the warplog from my arms and lifted

Bubbles up to stare him in the face. "You're growing so well. All that yummy meat from my store, yes? It is so good for a growing boy."

I eyed the creature. I was pretty sure the only direction he was growing was *out*. But Bubbles licked both of his eyeballs in rapid succession and gave Matilda a sort of toothy smile, made less cute by the sharp teeth and acid drool.

She tucked him into her side, oblivious to it all. "I've been running low on scraps this week. Someone comes in every morning and buys the previous day's cuttings. I'm not sure what they're feeding, but I've saved the very best piece for you, of course."

I creased my brow. We'd never had issues getting spoiled meat from Matilda's shop. It was the first I'd heard of anyone else buying up scraps.

"Do you know who's buying the old meat?" I asked. Flashes of shadow dogs gnawing on green cow legs ran through my mind.

Matilda pulled out a chunk of bone from some mystery creature and carefully unwrapped the thick paper with one hand. Bubbles watched her work intently, smacking his lips. "It's a woman. She comes nearly every morning before sunrise."

"Do you know her? Is she local?"

"I hadn't seen her before."

"Hm." I made the statement flat. If someone was suddenly feeding a pack of Shadow-Beasts, they'd probably also be new customers to a butcher's shop. I bit my lip. I didn't even know if the Shadow-Beasts needed to eat.

"Here you are, love." Matilda set Bubbles on the countertop and held the leg up. A tinted green hue colored the meat, and the slightest hint of decay bled from the flesh.

Bubbles' eyes widened. He opened his mouth up, and up, and up, until his skin stretched around the gaping hole where rivers of acid saliva pooled. Matilda tossed the rotten leg into the warplog's mouth. He didn't care that the limb doubled his body size. It disappeared into his maw, which clamped shut with all those pointy teeth. A moment later, Bubbles burped and closed his eyes—content.

I scooped the sleepy boy from the counter. He rolled in my arms until his tummy faced upward and all four limbs hung limp.

"You haven't heard of a murder at the university, have you?" I asked Matilda.

"You know I avoid news and gossip." She conjured a butcher's knife from somewhere and pointed the tip at me.

I sighed. "I know, but I have to ask."

Matilda winked at me. "Good luck to you, Rae. And Rae's friend."

I paused at the edge of my turn. Eyeing the giant mystery beast Matilda casually stuffed into Bubbles' mouth made me realize that she probably knew a lot about different kinds of animals—including some that may have gray fur. Even if all she told me was that it likely belonged to Magnolia's cat.

"One more question. If I brought in a sample of animal fur, would you be able to identify it?"

Her sharp gaze studied me. I thought the lines of her brow softened for a moment. Maybe she empathized with the town's Investigation Expert, or maybe she really liked Bubbles and tolerated me for his sake.

Finally, she shrugged. "Perhaps, but you'd be better off going to the North Gate Butcher. Archi raises a greater . . . variety of stock, so to speak. We deal with the same ol' here. And North

Gate gets interesting visitors with unusual requests."

"Thanks, Matilda." I let the true gratuity seep into my voice before heading toward the door.

Suzie followed me out of the store. "Did Bubbles just eat something bigger than he is?"

"I try not to ask questions," I said, glancing back. I might need to park Brew near the shop tomorrow and keep track of anyone unusual buying a lot of old meat, or maybe take it over to the North Gate and ask them some questions about the fur sample.

When I looked ahead, someone stood in front of me. I tried to backpedal, but it was too late.

I collided with Fraya's shoulder. She stumbled, and the bird at her side let out a loud squawk. I thought it tensed for a moment, then the woman pulled its leash, and the noise cut off.

"Sorry!" I clutched her elbow and pulled her upright. She coughed but straightened.

Silence settled. She wore shaded spectacles over her eyes and a black fabric twisted into her hair. Her clothes still looked immaculate, obviously expensive by the shape and flow of the garments. Fraya studied me before giving a small smile.

"Ah, Rae. I was hoping to see you soon, though perhaps not quite like this."

"I wasn't paying attention . . . hey, wasn't he red last time?" I gestured to the animal at her side.

The giant bird, which I distinctly remembered being a vivid red at our last appointment, bore rich, sapphire blue feathers. Even the base where its beak blended into the feathers was stained the color. It curled its toes, digging talons into the cobblestones.

Fraya didn't even glance at him. "He may have been. He changes colors based on his mood. But I'm much more interested in your investigation. Have you discovered anything else?"

I pursued my lips. The correct answer would be informing Fraya that I couldn't release information about an ongoing investigation. But she was technically helping us, even if that help hadn't been very fruitful yet.

"No." I heard the disappointment in my tone. "I thought we had a lead, but it ended up being nothing."

"Ah." A light faded from her eyes.

I scratched the back of my neck. "I still need to talk to the mortician, but we're close to the Sheriff's Station. Do you have time to look at the magic cast now?"

"The mortician?" Her tone perked up. "Now *that* sounds interesting. Is it very far? I shall accompany you there, after I buy some meat for my pet."

I opened my mouth, but the woman and bird stepped passed us and disappeared into Matilda's shop with the ring of a bell.

I snapped my jaw closed. A buzz of frustration caught in my chest. I didn't need Fraya to come to the morgue with me, I needed her to interpret the magic cast. But I also didn't want to risk angering her and abandoning the case completely.

Suzie looked over my shoulder. "I think we know where all the meat is going."

Sure enough, Fraya put a stack of coins on the counter and Matilda lugged a package of meat from the back, easily three times the size of the leg Bubbles had eaten. Fraya watched with careful eyes while Matilda cut the wrappings away to expose a plethora of bits and pieces of chopped meat.

The bird ate it all.

My voice refused to work as Suzie and I gaped at the sight. Without a break, the creature flicked one slice after another into its sharpened beak. Even Matilda turned a little green. Barely a minute passed, and the meat was gone.

I snapped my jaw shut. At least I could eliminate Fraya from trying to feed a pack of Shadow-Beasts.

Fraya and her pet excited the shop as though the creature at her side couldn't have devoured us in a handful of seconds. She gave a bright smile.

"The morgue now?"

* * *

Alivia was much too happy to have so many visitors in her morgue. She'd abandoned the usual black mask she wore, leaving her sculpted face bare and sharp. A long cloak hung to the floor. It concealed her feet enough to give the sense that she floated through her domain, where the dead stayed, caught between life and rest. I didn't know if ghosts existed, but I imagined that Alivia would be thrilled if any of her previous attendees haunted her.

"Rae." Her tone held an imitation of sincerity. "A pleasure to see you again." She did cast a flat look at the bird, which Fraya refused to leave upstairs, where I'd secured Bubbles so he wouldn't attempt to eat any of the corpses.

I nodded in reply. Suzie rubbed her arms as she glanced at the stacks of human-like shapes wrapped in loose white sheets. The morgue was nestled underground, naturally chilled, in addition to layers of cooling spells the students from the college cast regularly. A series of mirrors cascaded from the upper entrance, each carrying another beam of light to illuminate the autopsy table.

"I see you've brought friends?" Alivia's voice held the right amount of warmth, but it lacked depth. It could have been the waves roaring in the sea as much as a real, human voice.

"This is Marshal Leof's daughter, Suzie." I tugged her forward, which seemed to shock her focus away from the piles of bodies at the edges of the room.

"And this is—"

"Fraya," the woman said before I finished the introduction. She gave a little bow, which surprised me. "It is an honor to be in your morgue." Fraya paused, not long enough for me to shake off the discomfort from the gesture. "Can we see her?"

Alivia blinked. It didn't appear to be a sign of concern at the bizarre question, but more that she'd experienced an emotion she hadn't felt in a long time—one which startled her.

The mortician's lips peeled away from brilliant white teeth. "You wish to see the murder victim?"

Fraya nodded. "If it wouldn't be a burden."

"That's not necess—" I stammered.

Alivia waved my words away with a swift brush of her hand. She glided to one of the piles of white bodies and flicked through the parchment tags tied around each one.

Suzie shifted. "I'm not sure I want to see her."

I didn't either. It had been bad enough seeing Magnolia when she'd been freshly dead. Decay, even in the cold, changed someone.

"You can go upstairs," I said.

"I . . . I want to try. I think I'll be okay."

I could have urged her to leave the morgue, but being a

Crime Investigation Expert meant doing unpleasant things. Some of the most important tasks in the world involved being uncomfortable, knowing they were for the good of all in the end. Suzie could decide after this if she really wanted me to teach her the ways of death—and magic.

Alivia heaved a body from the top of a pile and discarded it like so much trash onto the morgue floor.

"Ohhh." Suzie sighed softly behind me.

I spun, just in time to see her skin turn green, then white, as her eyes rolled into her head. Her body softened with unconsciousness, heading straight for the ground. I didn't even want to know what disgusting things had touched that stone floor.

A groan escaped my lips as I caught Suzie in my arms. Thankfully, Bubbles was upstairs, or I may have dropped him to catch her. My muscles whined, but all the training with Tyfin had improved my strength. They barely shook with the woman's weight.

I hadn't noticed Alivia until she appeared beside me. Her cloudy gaze studied Suzie's still form with what I suspected was amusement.

"Here." The mortician thrust a cotton wad into my hands. "Break it."

I followed her directives, with a sneaking suspicion that if Suzie passed out alone down here, she may have found herself on the autopsy table.

Fragile glass snapped inside the wad, and the cotton exterior protected my fingers from the shards. Immediately, a putrid odor seeped into my nostrils. I gasped, the need to breathe competing with the desire to avoid the stench.

"What is that?"

"Scenting salts." Alivia snatched it from my hand and waved it before Suzie's nose. I wanted to throw up just thinking about the sulfur and ammonia being that close to her face. "The smell is known to revive victims of minor unconsciousness."

Sure enough, Suzie stirred a moment later. Alivia pulled the salts away, silently slipping back to Fraya's side near the bodies.

"What happened?" she asked, pressing a hand to her head.

"You passed out when Alivia moved the bodies."

"Ugh, don't remind me." She found her feet and only staggered for a moment. "I don't think I can stay down here."

I gave her a reassuring smile. "You're allowed to dislike things, Suzie. You can still make an impression on this world without being the toughest fool in the room."

Suzie hesitated for a moment, then grimaced at me before returning to the stairs. I bit my bottom lip, sort of wishing I could follow her. Her steps faded and a happy greeting that must have been Bubbles told me when she'd make it upstairs.

I wrinkled my nose as Alivia returned to her tenants. She tugged at the next sheet, and I saw Magnolia's name scrawled in perfect, thick, black handwriting across the tied parchment slip where the feet must have been. Alivia's brow creased as she handled the remains, an uncharacteristic frown bending her delicate features.

I stiffened. "What's wrong?"

"I'm sure it's nothing," she whispered.

Fraya stepped near the feet, bare hands out to catch the bottom of Magnolia's body. But the shape of the bundle wasn't quite right. It didn't move together. The section in Alivia's hands bent separately from where Fraya tried to grab the feet.

"Stop," I said, too quiet, too late.

The wrappings unbound. Alivia shrieked as gray and black

ash tumbled from the sheet and swirled across her pristine floor. Shards of charred bones fell next, accumulating into a macabre pile between the women's feet.

The ash carried an unholy smell of fire and damnation as what remained of Magnolia crawled its way up my nose.

My stomach coiled. I forced bile back down my throat.

If I'd had any doubt that the Shadow-Beasts were involved in Magnolia's murder, they all vanished in that moment. If Valen hadn't rescued me with his mysterious salve, I would be the burnt dust scattered in the wind. Suzie would too. I was glad she'd left and never had to picture her own skin and bones turned to fine powder.

I wanted to cover my eyes and scream, but the grainy feel of ash on my skin told me that Magnolia's remains had blown over my skin.

Alivia, her yelps completed, blinked up at me.

"She didn't look like that last time I saw her," she said, as though considering it absurd that she may have previously missed that detail.

"Send a messenger to Leof immediately." I backpedaled, keeping my gaze on that pile as though it may turn into a Shadow-Beast itself and chase after me. "I—I have to be somewhere."

My ankle banged into the first stair. The pain ran beneath the shock and fear, hardly felt at all. I glanced down to find my footing, then scrambled up several steps before looking back.

Both Alivia and Fraya leaned over the ash. Whatever horror had emerged from the bag must have faded from them. They conversed quietly, a slight smile shared between the pair.

I paused. The two of them whispering about what used to be a human being—no sign of despair or sympathy on their faces chilled me more than the ash on my hands. Alivia's gray eyes flashed at something Fraya said.

The bird turned to me. From the core of its iris, the sapphire blue faded, twisting and warping into a dark black, the color of shadows, of mourning.

Fraya jerked the leash, and he turned from me.

I finished the climb.

"Grab Bubbles," I told Suzie, holding my hands out as though they burned. "We've got to go."

Chapter 20

"How're you doing?" I passed Krissa a mug of steaming hot tea through the bars of her cell. I'd kept it simple—a classic black tea with extra sugar and honey because my friend had a sweet tooth.

She accepted the drink but gave a slight shrug. "I've stayed in better places."

I twisted my fingers around the hem of my tunic. The prison cells were beneath the Sheriff's Station in a sort of 'out of sight, out of mind' location. There weren't any windows to offer sunlight, so rows of torches lined the blank wall before the cells. Krissa's regular view was the whitewashed stone wall directly across the way.

An awkward silence settled between us. I opened and closed my mouth a couple of times, waiting for the words to come out. But I didn't know what to say.

"I'm sorry," I said, the same time Krissa said, "It's all my fault you're down here."

We made eye contact and paused. The silence turned from tension to something more soothing.

Krissa laughed, a genuine, throaty sound that mismatched the prison. "Why are *you* sorry? You're not involved at all."

"I'm sorry I haven't solved this case yet to be able to get you out of here. Why did you say it's all your fault? You *didn't* kill Magnolia, right?"

She waved her hand. "Of course not. I'd never use magic to do something like that. The probability of discovery is so high, plus it's harder to dispose of any unwanted witnesses, should one arise. No, I'd try something more subtle. Maybe poison or pushing my victim in front of a wagon."

"How is pushing someone in front of a wagon more subtle than magic?" I raised a brow.

"If there's no witnesses."

Her gaze faded where I knew she imagined the two scenarios and worked out which has the best likelihood of her getting away with the crime. But I felt a grin crawl across my face.

"I can't believe you're trapped in a prison cell and making jokes about committing murder."

"Well, I am imagining a lot of people dead right now, starting with that damn Castor." She clenched her fist and shook it toward the ceiling above. "As soon as I'm out of here, I'm pushing that constable into the biggest wagon I can find." She dropped her hand to look at me. "Besides, terrible things can happen in life to anyone at any time. You can either stand strong through them, trust those closest to you, and thrive, or watch as all your problems slowly drown you."

I bit my lip. An ache beat inside my chest seeing my best friend find such courage at a low moment.

"You said Tyfin's coming so you can do training down here?" Krissa changed the subject, and I swiped a tear from the corner of my eyes, hoping she didn't notice.

"Yeah, he said skipping training isn't an option in my line of work."

"Making tea?"

"I think he meant the 'investigating potentially dangerous crimes committed by potentially dangerous criminals' part."

Krissa tapped her chin. "Ah. Speaking of dangerous criminals, tell me how the investigation into my case is going."

I sank onto the stone floor and gave her all the updates—confidentiality be damned.

* * *

"Fifty-one. Fifty-two. Fifty-three." Krissa's voice comforted me more than I thought possible. Despite the sweat beading on my face and the air stretching my lungs, the normalcy of her counting while I did one of the horrible crunch exercises Tyfin demanded soothed some of the knots in my gut.

My sword fighting trainer didn't appear uncomfortable in the depths of the prison below the Sheriff's Station. I'd try to tell Tyfin that I couldn't train this week. I'd explained about Krissa being wrongfully imprisoned and only one full day remained before the Sheriff would hold a trial. The man had blinked at me.

"Will your enemies stop an assault because your life has suddenly become unfair?" he'd asked. "Would an assassin cease to kill you out of *pity*?"

I'd almost inquired exactly *what* assassin was trying to kill me, and if he knew something I didn't, but my resolve whittled away. The exercise did steady my mind. And the helpless feeling I'd experienced at the hands of the Providers faded every time I practiced with my sword.

And I'd killed two Shadow-Beasts, one with the blade. I wanted to do that again and again. Well—not exactly that—but to improve my abilities and be confident in them.

So, I did more curls on the hard prison floor, with only unnatural torchlight illuminating the space, and Krissa counting each rep for me.

"Fifty-six, fifty-seven. So, the scent map from the harloon sample didn't match the one on Matilda's body? Fifty-eight." I was pretty sure that Krissa's questions made her counting inaccurate.

"They didn't match at all," I hissed between breaths. "The fur probably belonged to Magnolia's cat, anyway." But I needed to talk to the North Gate Butcher like Matilda suggested. My to-do list felt never-ending.

"Bummer." Krissa slouched onto her thin mattress and the old wooden frame complained. She wore a plain linen tunic and matching breeches. A bucket of water and the mattress were all that adorned her prison cell. "Sixty. Sixty-one."

I stopped the curls. She kept counting without looking.

"Sixty-two. Sixty-three."

"I've finished," I said.

"Oh." She blinked. "And Magnolia's body turned to *ash*? In the morgue? How?"

"I don't know. Either she sustained an injury from the Shadow-Beasts before she died, or they'd somehow gotten into the morgue after her death."

"Sucks either way." Krissa crossed her arms beneath her head.

"Now for the sword," Tyfin said, as though it were another day in the sparring ring and not in a dungeon that smelled suspiciously like piss.

I sighed and picked up the wooden weapon.

Tyfin shook his head. "No. If you've killed with the blade, then it's time to train with it."

I paused and eyed the weapon in question. The silver short sword rested against the stone wall. I'd cleaned it after killing the creature, but a faint hint of steam seemed to seep from the metal.

Krissa sat up. "Now this, I have to watch."

I glanced at Tyfin. He chuckled, probably at the shock and fear on my face. My teacher grabbed the sword and pulled it from the sheath. He crossed to me, picked up my hand, and placed the hilt in my palm.

"You're ready, Rae," he said.

I waited for disagreeing words to surface. Instead, a cool confidence, almost as icy as Valen's rage, stirred at my center. I closed my fingers around the hilt and nodded to Tyfin. I *was* ready.

"Start at upper guard."

Tyfin backed up to give me more space. The narrow hallway offered little room. If my movements became sloppy, I'd run the sword into the stone wall. Even more reason not to be sloppy.

I closed my eyes and drew a deep breath. The weapon felt good in my palm. I cradled it firmly, but gently, enough to hold it tight without sacrificing any flexibility in my wrists. My left hand grabbed the lower part of the hilt, giving me balance and strength.

I drew the sword over my head. It weighed more than the wooden blades.

It felt right.

"First drill," Tyfin said. His voice faded into the back of my mind, to a darker place I'd never been before. The sword rested over my head, the new strength in my arms preventing any misdirection, cutting a line down my center, to my very self. "Strike."

It cut through the air in a breathtaking flurry. My legs moved with muscle memory, setting up the next motion before Tyfin called.

"Front guard."

I stepped back and pulled my hands close to my face, the sharpened tip pointed out toward an opponent's face.

"Strike."

I swung down, but really the sword and I moved together. It became a part of me, an extension of my arms. I knew exactly where the blade would streak as I directed the cut. I knew when I grew too close to the cell bars or the torches flickering on the walls.

My magic awoke as I moved, as though each step were a part of an enchantment I'd never learned. It licked along the sword's edge, where the metal had cut into the Shadow-Beast, and released more of that thick smoke.

It wasn't from the beasts at all—it was from me.

"Mid guard. Strike. Low guard. Strike."

We *moved*—the sword and I. When Tyfin finished with the guards, he moved onto the strikes. My feet stepped and glided. I wondered if this was how Alivia felt when she moved around her morgue, in her own domain, where magic, life, and strength collided.

I couldn't stop. I didn't want to stop. My magic hummed and sang, but the real power was the strength each movement empowered inside me.

I was strong.

Strike.

I could defend myself.

Strike.

Nobody could hurt me.

Strike.

Nobody could hurt anyone I loved.

Strike.

Sweat dripped from my body when I finally stopped and opened my eyes. My chest heaved. There wasn't enough of the musty air down here to satisfy my need for oxygen. Tyfin leaned against the wall, arms crossed, a smug look on his face.

"What?" I wheezed breathlessly.

"I hadn't said anything for over ten minutes. I stopped calling the positions, and you ran through your own drill, Rae. On your own."

"And it was awesome," Krissa added.

A blush lit my cheeks. Sticky salt dried on my skin, but I didn't care.

I had done it.

"That was a good start. Let's make some adjustments for you to practice before we meet again. Back to upper guard."

Tyfin walked me through the drill, tweaking my arm and leg positions as he saw fit. When I repeated the initial series of steps to his satisfaction, he gave me a stern nod.

"I'll see you next week."

"You're a badass," Krissa said after Tyfin disappeared up the stairs and I plopped into a damp blob on the ground outside of her cell. "An absolute badass."

I still couldn't breathe, but a wide smile curled my lips.

Chapter 21

Brew purred in the fresh rays of sunshine, happy to be back to a day of somewhat normalcy. Green leaves rustled overhead in a slight breeze and the sound of visitors chatting as they entered through Hallow's Promise's North Gate drifted across the wind. Wildflowers emitted an enchanting scent over the clear day.

And I was grumpy.

Today marked the last full day I could investigate Krissa's case before the Sheriff arrived from the capital. Depending what time he entered town, the trial could be tomorrow, or the next day. Justice didn't wait, which was why I'd parked Brew outside of the North Gate, directly across from the butcher's shop in that side of town. If they thought it at all possible to identify where the fur came from, I'd march them straight to Leof's office.

But the bills didn't wait either.

Working part time for Leof certainly helped keep my finances afloat, but Brew provided my primary source of income. The supplement meant I could take off a few sparse days—certainly not regularly. It also meant that I couldn't talk to the butcher until I'd sold a few drinks to cover another day's expenses.

My sour mood exposed itself through the menu I'd thrown together before departing.

"What exactly does the Anxie-TEA do?" A short, redheaded woman squinted at the sign perched on the side of the wagon. My handwriting pressed a bit too hard into the chalkboard and scratched the words into the wood. I'd have to repaint it when I wanted to change the menu.

"Anxie-TEA is a milder flavor. It's a little bitter, but there's a healthy dose of sweetening syrups I could add to dull that. It's also infused with a bit of magic to promote soothing feelings."

She nodded slightly. "And the Sus-SIP-sion?"

"That one will subtly discourage any unwanted visitors from making an appearance around you. The drink itself is fairly basic with a floral base, but the magic emits an unpleasant feeling when anyone you dislike approaches."

"Which would you recommend?" she asked.

I clenched my teeth. "Is there anyone you dislike that's bothering you?"

"Not really."

"Then how about the Anxie-TEA? It'll give you a lovely feeling to enjoy this beautiful day."

She gave me a bright smile, which unknotted some of the tension in my gut and remolded it into guilt. I'd opened Brew-Tea-Ful to use my magic to help the residents of Hallow's Promise in exchange for hiding my identity from the capital. I had no reason to be bitter toward my customers.

"It'll be just a moment," I said in a softer tone.

Brew creaked as I pulled out my supplies. I patted the countertop.

"I know, I know. I'll be nicer next time." Maybe I needed some Anxie-TEA.

Brew flipped open a rear cupboard, and I pulled out the jar of loose tea leaves. I spooned a few into a small, metal dish and pressed it down with a thick rod. The herbs formed a tight puck, which would allow the water to cover a greater surface area during pouring, enhancing the flavors of the chamomile and hops.

We didn't have enough evidence in Krissa's case with how little information we'd gathered. The tuft of fur from Magnolia's body was likely from her cat—though I would confirm with the butcher after my shift. The magic cast was waiting for Fraya's interpretation, but she seemed hesitant to commit to the task. Castor had that cursed letter he'd found in Krissa's home, which someone must have planted, but he refused to allow me to investigate it.

Steam billowed from the small cauldron over the small, inset oven. I balanced the pressed tea over a new mug and slowly drizzled the water into the puck. Drops filtered through, an off-yellow liquid with hints of green. They fell into the bottom of the cup with a slight plop sound.

No fingerprints at the crime scene. A failed scent map to Dean Parthum's harloon. I had nothing—less than nothing. I was almost out of my most valuable resource—time.

I leaned my head out the sash. "What flavors do you want?"

"Do you have anything sort of sweet but not too . . . bright?"

"Mapel it is."

I ducked back inside. Brew opened the syrup cupboard for me.

"Thanks."

I poured some syrup along the top of the herb puck. It settled above the damp leaves before sinking through the crevices. When I poured the next bit of water, the maple melted into the liquid and released a sweet, earthy smell.

Whoever committed the crime knew Krissa well enough to plant evidence at her house, and that she had applied for the Board of Professional Standards. Magnolia had a cat that ran away after her death. Someone else had hired Valen to investigate in murder. None of these brought me any closer to a suspect.

Across the way, a sliver of motion danced in the sunlight. The North Gate butcher shop's door slipped open, and a young woman walked out, her blonde hair in a thick braid. She wore a simple brown dress with a black linen apron and headed straight for Brew.

I spilt the last of the water onto the counter and hissed as scalding splashes jumped onto my skin. The butcher was on her way over here, and I hadn't even prepared what to ask her.

"Here you go." I carefully handed over the hot mug of Anxie-TEA. "Sip it slowly, or the effects can diminish too quickly."

"Thank you." The customer handed over her coins, cradled the drink with both hands, and sipped a bit from the top. Her shoulders sagged in relief.

Brew settled around me. The wagon loved seeing happy, fulfilled customers as much as I did.

But I also needed to figure out Magnolia's true killer, and quickly.

The young woman finished crossing the street and perched across the sash to study the menu.

"Can I help you choose a drink?" I asked, putting on my most friendly smile and hoping there weren't any herbs caught in my teeth. I didn't want to scare her away before asking about the fur sample.

"I'm a little curious about the difference between the STIR-crazy and the Uncertain-TEA?"

I flinched at how deary the menu turned out today. "How about I make you something off the menu that's perfect for such a beautiful day? I also see you came from the butcher's store across the street. I'll infuse a bit of magic that may bring a higher chance of financial success for the day—on the house, of course."

Her eyes shimmered. "Wow, that would be so generous of you."

"I'm always happy to support local businesses." I pulled a tall glass from the shelf and filled it with ice from Brew's chilled cupboard. Bubbles groaned when I pushed him over a bit to open the door. I eyed the warplog wearily. He'd burp up the bone from yesterday and start gnawing it to shreds at any moment, and I wanted him outside the wagon when that happened.

"Do you like working at the shop?" I asked. "I'm sorry, I didn't catch your name."

"Celeste. And it's my father's shop, but he claims to be old and frail and makes me run it most days." She rolled her eyes. "He doesn't seem particularly frail when old lady Helga from down the street shows up in the store and he all but sprints to the front."

I laughed, a surprised, genuine sound. "Do you see a wide assortment of animals? Would you be able to identify a creature from a piece of fur or hair?"

Celeste pressed her lips together. "That's an odd question. I'm really not sure anyone's ever asked me that. We do see a few exotic animals since visitors bring their hunts in from the woods to be cut and packaged. Why do you ask?"

I didn't answer right away as I dropped fresh cut strawberries, mint leaves, and a lemon wedge into the bottom of the glass. I carefully pressed a thick wooden rod against the ingredients and focused on turning them into a pulp while I formulated an answer.

"To be honest, it's not a coincidence that I'm here today. I was planning to visit your store after my shift."

"Oh, do you have a mysterious beast for us to carve up? Even if I'm unfamiliar with it, my father knows much more."

Once the juices combined, I added a healthy spoonful of wild honey and mixed them all once more time with the rod. Sweetness and spicy mint overwhelmed the wagon.

"It's nothing quite like that. I'm employed to investigate the murder of a professor at the college. I've been told this shop may have knowledge about a piece of fur we found at the crime scene."

Celeste's face paled. "Magnolia?" she whispered. Her round eyes and lips spread in a wide circle said she hadn't known about the death. "She hasn't been here in days. She's . . . gone?"

"I—Did you know her?"

"She bought fresh meat every week for her . . ." Celeste glanced over her shoulder, a sudden tension stiffening her frame. I looked back too, wondering if she sensed danger in the woods. Not even the shadows danced. I dumped the chilled green tea into her drink and reached to pass it through the window, but Celeste leaned into the sash and lowered her voice.

"Where is her cat?"

I froze. I didn't remember mentioning Magnolia's name, and I certainly hadn't mentioned the cat.

I leaned toward her and matched my tone to hers. "It's missing."

She visually recoiled. "You'll need to talk to my father. He will know what's best to say and to leave unsaid."

I didn't want to leave anything unsaid, but a hint of danger warped Celeste's words.

"When?" I asked instead.

"Now," Celeste answered. "If the cat is missing, then sooner is better."

* * *

Mr. Haverhill, Celeste's father, looked how I expected a grumpy old man to look. He had thin, white hair, a rustle of beard across his wrinkled face, and age spots up and down his arms. But he also had an axe slung through a loop on his belt and studied me with the wisdom only age and many mistakes can produce. It didn't matter that he smelled like old cheese, or his shoes had holes in each toe. It mattered that he knew about Magnolia.

He studied me. Haverhill's gaze felt like standing too close to a roaring fire. One false move could snap me up, but it was rather warm and pleasant until then.

Finally, he grunted and gave a half nod. Celeste's shoulders sagged, which I took to be a sign of relief that I'd passed some sort of test. She lifted the sweet citrus tea to her lips and gave me a startled, pleasant smile.

"My girl tells me you're asking about Magnolia." He pulled a pipe from a table near his chair and fiddled open a tin of some kind of dark powder. "You shouldn't do that."

I leaned back in my chair. The rear of the butcher's shop

was mostly square if I didn't squint at the back wall too hard. Sparse, but well-selected furniture adorned the room. Haverhill claimed the most comfortable looking seat—a plush cream armchair with deep mahogany carvings along the legs. He tapped his shoes on the tile floor, holes and all.

"Sir, Magnolia's life was taken away from her. That's not something I can simply ignore."

That sharp gaze returned. "And why not?"

I opened my mouth, then snapped it shut again. There were a lot of reasons I'd turned to investigating crimes and researching better ways to solve them. My magic called to death, and though I couldn't choose my power, I could embrace all the opportunities it presented. That was reason enough to do this job.

But that wasn't the real reason.

I've felt injustice. I've tasted true evil in the hands of the king and his Providers. I knew what it felt like to have all options stripped away and the part of my soul that was magic used for cruelty.

If I could do anything to prevent another child—person—from feeling anything close to that, or make an offender answer for their crimes, then that was why I did it.

"If someone brings darkness into another person's world," I answered Haverhill, my eyes locked on his, "they should answer for taking that light away."

He smiled, just a hint. "Magnolia would have liked you." I wasn't sure that was a compliment. "I'm not going to explain the mess Magnolia got herself into with the college and the cult she was involved in, or whatever. You must know all that by now, or you wouldn't be here." By 'cult,' he must have meant the Board of Professional Standards. "But those people gave

Magnolia a curse disguised as a gift."

"What was it?"

"A Nightingale."

I shook my head. "I'm not familiar with that."

"Good. No one should be. They're powerful, proud beasts that remain in the most elusive parts of the world. It's rumored only gods or devils can find one. But Magnolia made a wish, and that cult gave her a Nightingale."

"I still don't understand."

Celeste took another loud sip of her drink as her father continued. "I've seen a Nightingale once in my life before Magnolia's. It took the form of a great snake and split the world in half to release smoke demons from the depths."

I raised my brows. A smoke demon sounded a lot like a Shadow-Beast.

"My pa sold the owner one of our best bulls from the field. The stranger took the bull and the Nightingale out of the gates and the demons followed. You see, the Nightingale controls the demons, and the owner controls the Nightingale."

"Why did the Board of Professional Standards give Magnolia a Nightingale instead of fulfilling her wish for healing?"

Celeste put a hand on her father's shoulder and answered. "The Nightingales emit a high-pitched sound inaudible to our ears but able to split the fragments of space itself. Life and death, sickness, and health don't exist in a space of nothingness. The board believed Magnolia could wield that ability and discover how to harvest it into our world. If illness can't exist, everyone would be forever healed."

"But splitting into space is dangerous." Haverhill's voice sounded hard and worn, like he'd had the same discussion before. "Nobody knows where the Nightingale opens. It may be nothingness, or the depths of hell and devils."

"And they are shape-changers." Celeste swirled her drink and watched the fruity chunks bleed red into the tea. "Depending on the current owner's personality, they will alter their shape to the best match. Magnolia's Nightingale, Whiskers, looked like a common house cat. Gray, long fur, very friendly. For all its power, I believed it truly liked her."

A chill ran down my spine. "It changes shape based on its owner? So, it could be any animal right now?"

Celeste and Haverhill both nodded.

His cracked voice sent chills down my spine. "Many who obtain a Nightingale find death at the hands of another. Their power is immense, unspeakable. We need to find it before someone learns how to use its power to summon terrible beings—and who knows what else."

I bit my lip. The Nightingale had already sung, at least twice, and released Shadow-Beasts into Hallow's Promise.

I had no idea what it would do next.

Chapter 22

The area around Hallow's Promise had its share of magical beings that liked to sneak into town and wreak havoc on the residents. But other creatures resided inside the walls that hadn't—or couldn't be—relocated during the town's development. These beings were old, powerful, and terrifying. They didn't bother emerging from the depths of the darkness of the forest, and if they ever did, the townsfolk assumed the apocalypse would follow.

These creatures resided in The Void—a dense cluster of trees just below the North Gate where sunlight refused to penetrate and strange sounds in the night encouraged pedestrians to walk faster.

I loved The Void. Whatever power blessed or cursed the land made it the perfect place for secret discussions without being overheard.

Valen, Leof, and I stood inside Brew. I'd never considered the wagon small before, but I questioned its size with the mercenary and marshal in such a close proximity. Their blatant hatred of each other, combined with Valen's delicious scent of autumn and spice, made me forget what to say next. I'd told Suzie to stay home and rest, and deeply regretted that decision.

I could have used a human shield between the two.

I worked a loaf of bread on the countertop, kneading it like I wanted to push it through the wood and into the depths of the wagon.

"Magnolia's body turned to ash, which makes you think the Shadow-Beasts are involved in the murder?"

"They *are* involved," I told Leof, rolling the dough again. "The Nightingale can call them whenever its owner wishes. It is no coincidence Magnolia was murdered, her mythical beast stolen, and then her body disintegrated."

He put his hands up. "I'm not arguing with you."

I pressed my lips together. As sunshine faded to night, my time to solve the murder and set Krissa free grew slim. If the Sheriff arrived tomorrow and put her to trial, I'd do anything to let my friend keep her freedom—but I'd rather find a peaceful solution.

I spread the dough over the floured countertop and pushed along the edges with my fingertips until it stretched and softened into a thin rectangle. Thick globs of butter peppered the dough, followed by a generous mix of sugar, brown sugar, and cinnamon. The spicy sweet smells soothed some of the tension from both men inside the wagon.

"I couldn't find Fraya Hawkthorne today." Valen leaned against the cupboard near me. He pretended not to watch my hands as I rolled the bread and trapped all that goodness inside, but I felt his gaze on me. Heat spread through me despite the approaching night. "The gate guards said a woman matching her description returned through the South Gate before midday, but the trail went cold after that."

"We also haven't figured out the connection with Irabel's disappearance yet." I tucked in the corners of the roll.

"Maybe there isn't a connection. Dean Perthum seemed convinced she'd just left out of anger again." Leof reached for a pinch of the dough, and I smacked his hand. He gave a mischievous grin as he drew away.

"I know where Fraya's staying. If she won't come do the magic cast comparison at the Station, I'll have to bring it to her. And now we know the scent map from the fur at the crime scene will match the Nightingale—if we can locate it and get a sample."

I set the dough into a bread pan and slipped it atop the glowing coals in the fire. A spark of magic popped within me when the heat soaked through, and the bread began to rise.

"It sounds like you've got it all worked out." The mercenary's voice was all honey and sweet wine and made me grind my teeth. "What do you need us for, Sunshine?"

"As much as I hate admitting it, I'm not sure I could take down any more Shadow-Beasts." At least, not without exposing my magic, signaling the king my exact location. Then, I wouldn't have to worry about Krissa's trial or Valen's annoying nicknames, because they'd be dead. "I'm hoping you can help me with that."

"I'd be happy to protect you, Rae." Leof added a bit of a bite at the end of my name.

But I shook my head. If I kept grinding my teeth, I was going to get a headache. "I haven't had much time to talk about the Shadow-Beasts at the park, Leof, but they weren't there for me. One of the creatures looked right at me and turned away."

His brow creased, a troubled look clouding his head. "What are you saying?"

"They were there for Suzie. I think you found something really close to the murderer and they tried to weaken you through your daughter. It'll be better if you're with Suzie in public in case they try something like that again."

Which left Valen with me.

I didn't look at him. I really didn't. But the smile that spread across his face like wildfire burned too bright for me to ignore.

"Say it, Sunshine."

I bit the tip of my tongue to keep from grinding my teeth too hard.

"Valen," I wished the words were a killing spell, ones to stop his annoying heart from one beat to the next, "I need your help."

The simmering heat and anger between the three of us ramped up. A balanced flame paused at the edge of disaster, threatening to spill over all of us.

Valen laughed. The sound stole some of the tension. Even Brew sagged in a creaky relief. "I'll do anything you want me to."

I wanted to storm into The Void and find the first creature that could fit me whole into its mouth.

Instead, I rinsed out the dishes and waited for the bread to bake.

* * *

The two men talked quietly at the rear of the wagon, likely driven away from my rapidly fouling mood. I carefully shifted the bread pan from the coals. The heat of the metal and oven felt familiar, easing my mind slightly. Rich tendrils of bread and cinnamon swirled into my nose, also easing the frustration.

I flipped the pan over and the loaf plopped onto the counter. It needed to cool before I could slice it.

The two men suddenly reappeared at my side, beckoned by the promise of delicious food. I gave them my sternest look, and they kept a wider distance.

"Our biggest problem is that we're not going to recognize the Nightingale if we see it before Leof can get a sample for the scent." Valen crossed his arms. He watched as I picked up a large, serrated knife and set it against the loaf.

The edges bit into the bread and sliced into a thick section.

"That's what the bread is for," I said.

Valen's eyes widened as he felt the magic spilling from the first cut. The flour had grown in a cemetery at the edge of town, and I'd harvested it from hallowed ground myself. I'd enchanted the sugarcane and molasses from my own spell keeping stocks, and I purchased the cinnamon from a traveling vendor who refused to reveal its original location, but the jar brimmed with power. My touch of magic blended them together, giving it a new life.

Leof snatched a slice from the countertop and raised it toward his mouth.

I smacked it from his hand. "Don't eat it, it's magic bread."

The cinnamon sugar slice fell to the ground and bounced once. My eyes widened while I watched it land, and, from his cupboard, the warplog locked his gaze onto the food.

"Bubbles, no!" I yelled, reaching down for the slice, knowing I would be far, far too late.

Bubbles' eyes widened. He peeled back his lips and showed off razor teeth as he chomped the piece in one bite. He licked both of his eyeballs and nestled back into his cupboard.

We all stared at him.

"What does the magic bread do?" Leof asked in a hushed tone.

"It's supposed to reveal a being's true identity," I said. "I don't know exactly how."

Bubbles' eyes widened. He shifted. The warplog's stomach bulged. He cast a concerned look at me as he ballooned from his abdomen into a perfect circle with short arms and long legs. The bloating stretched his smooth skin until I feared it may pop.

Bubbles opened his mouth and let out a huge, loud burp.

Brew shook, either from disgust or from the actual force of Bubbles' burp. A foul smell of rotten meat and sharp acid escaped from the obscene amount of air fleeing the creature's mouth. It continued long enough for my jaw to drop and my eyes to grow dry as I forgot to blink.

Finally, he stopped.

A few noises responded from The Void, including several that sounded like the frantic sounds of an animal attempting to run away.

"Well," Valen blinked once at the warplog. "Looks like the bread works."

Chapter 23

The magic cast consumed most of the floor space inside Brew. Its delicate twists and twirls spiraled around in a detailed design. I wished I knew what it meant. Information, potentially the exact answer I needed, rested somewhere inside those curving spirals. But I hadn't studied the science of deciphering them . . . yet.

With the clay cast hogging all the room's available space, Valen and I stood near the rear door, very close together. I studied him from the corners of my eyes. He was large, in a sort of muscular, proportionate way. He wore a white buttoned tunic with a dark brown, worn leather jacket over the top. His black breeches tucked into hefty boots and smelled like cinnamon from the magic bread I'd distributed between the three of us. A longsword hung from a sheath off one hip. I knew if he drew the sword, it would be the larger twin to my own blade. The two were from the same set.

I used to hate the man—when he'd arrived in Hallow's Promise bearing a threat to me, my life, and the ones I cared for. I still hated him when he laughed at me from deep in his gut and when he said 'Sunshine' with just the wrong tone. But I didn't hate him all the time, not anymore, and those full lips and sparkling blue eyes and all that powerful energy made it hard to hate him at all.

Not when he made my heart skip so many beats.

He didn't even turn his head toward me. "Like what you see, Sunshine?"

A hot blush spread across my cheeks. I locked my gaze forward, refusing to give him the satisfaction of a response.

"Why are you even here?" I snapped.

"I told you. I've been hired to investigate Magnolia's murder."

"No, I mean why are you still around Hallow's Promise? There are large cities with plenty of jobs for a mercenary. Why did you stay here?"

His brow creased for a moment before he flattened it. "I have personal business in Hallow's Promise."

I snorted. "That's hardly an answer. You have a house here. You're picking up jobs that probably pay pennies compared to what you're used to. It doesn't make any sense."

He stepped toward me. The next sentence faded on my tongue, drowned by his warmth and scent. He tucked his index finger under my chin and pulled it up until we stared into each other's eyes.

"Why are you in Hallow's Promise, Sunshine? We both know you have power capable of wiping away the leaders of corruption in this kingdom. But you're here, with your magic wagon and your little frog. Why?"

Valen's blue eyes twinkled with a twist of amusement and sincerity.

"He's not a frog," I whispered.

My secrets bubbled from the depths of my memories. Krissa knew the full story of my past, and I suspected Leof had pieced together a few details. But the more people that knew, the more people would be in danger. The king would kill anyone who ever knew about me to protect the precious secret of my magic and what he used it for. "I can't use my magic. It's never helped anyone. I've only used it to hurt and kill."

His touch softened, and he ran his fingertips along the bottom of my jaw. "I've hurt and killed people too. It's not something to be done lightly, but if everyone is afraid to defend the weak and innocent, they are the ones who hurt the most."

I leaned toward him, hypnotized by his eyes. Our chests touched and his fingers trailed into my hair. I closed my eyes as tingles slid down my spine.

"Tell me what you've done, Sunshine." It was quiet, soothing, a request and not a demand.

And I was back in the capital, drawn there in my own mind, but it felt real enough that the chill in the memories sprouted bumps along my arms.

A wake of bodies filled the hallways of the castle. My weapon— the man who's will I'd claimed and stuffed with the lives of five people—walked in front of me. He'd stolen a sword from one of his —our—victims and rivets of red slid down the blade.

"This is the exit," I said.

He paused, the only indication that he listened at all. My magic coursing through his veins kept his mind and body from imploding with the power of all those lives. My heart sank. He wouldn't survive what I had done to him. Once the magic—me—left, he'd be unable to sustain himself. "There will be more guards waiting outside."

His head ducked, a barely visible sign of understanding. The Providers had shaved his head and tortured him before bringing him to me. Bruises lined his cheeks and exposed back. Cuts and slashes followed, a few obtained from our trek down the spire. I didn't know what color his eyes were because they'd turned black with my power.

The man pushed the doors open. The guards were there, armed and ready.

He cut them apart. I stood in the doorway and watched. His blade spun so fast, it turned into a silver blur, flinging blood and raindrops through the air. Some splashed onto the hem of my Provider's robe. I watched the drop soak into the fabric and turn invisible with the darkness.

That's what I wanted to be. Invisible.

The guards fell. More would take their place. I needed to leave before then.

My magic was fading. I could feel the strain as I tried to dredge up more and pour it into this man, to sustain him a little longer. The Providers had brought him to me to kill him and transfer his life to that of the decrepit king. Though he'd escaped that fate, I would be his death yet.

He turned and looked at me expectantly. My reflection moved in his eyes. His world was dark, except where I stood, and he waited for what I demanded next.

I dropped my gaze. Shame and rage burned inside me, but so did selfishness and survival. There were archers on the rooftops, but they wouldn't shoot me, not when the king depended on my magic to stay alive.

"I'm sorry," I told the stranger who had saved my life without choosing to. "I'm so sorry."

He tilted his head, giving me a view of another bruise along the side of his otherwise healthy cheek.

"Stay here." The tears on my cheeks mixed with the rain falling from the skin. I ran my sleeve over my face and embraced the scratch of the fabric on my skin. I deserved to be uncomfortable. I deserved far worse. But I said, "stay here."

I turned and walked toward the gates of the Capital. They slid open at my touch, the dagger tattoo burning slightly on my arm. I felt the gaze of archers on my back as they called for more guards, but I'd be as far as possible before they arrived.

I also felt the stranger watch me. He didn't follow—he couldn't, because I'd told him to stay. I'd taken him like a dog on a chain and left him even easier.

An awful sickness twisted in my gut. But I walked until my breathing steadied, then I ran.

And I was back with Valen, inside Brew, safe in Hallow's Promise. The goosebumps were gone, but my fingers still shook.

"I've hurt people that tried to help me. I tossed them aside without a second glance." The memories were old, but a tear fell from my eye and trailed across my cheek. When it touched the place where Valen's fingers rested on my face, a hot spark lit there. He brushed his fingers over it, erasing any evidence of its existence.

I thought we'd remain in that silence like we always did. The place where neither one of us takes a step forward.

But Valen spoke.

"I'm here for you, Sunshine, in Hallow's Promise." Valen said the words I'd wished for days ago. My heart pounded harder, and I felt his beat against my chest. "But you're not ready to know why."

I tensed and drew back to see his face better. An intensity lined his expression, tightened the corners of his eyes. I didn't know what he meant, but I knew it was important. For a moment, it wasn't just Valen looking at me. It was a mission, a hope, a familiar stranger.

"Who are you?" I asked. "Did I know you before all of this?"

Brew shook, letting us know we'd arrived at the Chopines,

as near to Fraya's house as the ley lines could get.

Valen dropped his hand from my face and pushed open the wagon door. "All mercenaries look the same, right, Sunshine?" He jumped from the step and studied the area, one hand on his sword.

I laughed, because I knew that's what he wanted, but I had many more questions I'd demand from the man before he finally left Hallow's Promise.

* * *

We walked through the Chopines, each of us carrying one side of the magic cast. The clay felt sturdy enough, but I still walked carefully and avoided anything suspiciously unstable on the street. I'd left several drawings of the cast at my office in the Station, but conclusions were always more accurate using the originals.

Valen's lip curled. "I've never liked this part of town."

Extravagant buildings rose on either side of us. Pristine flowers gave off the smell of gardenias and lilies. Even the cobblestones beneath my feet had been sanded level and cushioned my steps.

"Surely it's a good fit for a mercenary that brings in bags of money like you do."

He chuckled. "I'd love if you showed me where all those bags are. Let me know if this is too heavy for your little arms."

I snorted and grounded my teeth but considered his point. My arms *were* fine. The thick clay and awkward grip didn't strain my muscles at all. For all Tyfin's torture with the sword and conditioning, my body had gained considerable strength.

"The house Fraya's staying in is right up here." I ducked my head to the side.

The residents of the Chopines probably laughed at us from their windows. Many of them had likely never carried anything down the street—they'd hire someone to do it for them.

Finally, Fraya's house loomed before us. The golden stamps on the bricks looked less welcoming and more foreboding. Darkness leaked from the windows. No torches were lit. Nobody was home.

My heart sank. The Sheriff would be here in the morning. I needed answers tonight.

"The door," Valen said quietly. His stance had changed. The tender laughter faded away into a tight stance. He glanced around, taking in all the surroundings, a warrior waiting for the next attack.

The front door was ajar.

My throat tightened. Were we too late? Had the murderer realized Fraya's involvement in the case and beaten us to her?

"Let's put this down," Valen said. We lowered the magic cast onto the cushioned grass of the front lawn. He pulled his sword and advanced to the door. I pressed my lips together. I should have brought my sword.

The mercenary stood to the side and slid the door open. The marble soaked in the shadows, turning it into an inky blackness. Valen stepped inside and gestured for me to wait.

I waited. A knot tightened in my gut.

Valen returned. "It's empty."

I walked through the door and paused at the sight. The house was *empty*. All the grand furniture and artwork had been stripped from the walls. Gaping nothingness sat where the blue velvet couch had once been.

One item remained, misplaced among the architecture and emptiness. A single, vivid red feather rested in the center of the floor.

I knelt and picked it up. As my fingers pinched the stem, a muted grayness erupted from the tip and leeched away the ruby color of the feather. The gray spread up and up, and as it moved, the texture and shape of the feather changed too.

A moment later, the red feather I'd grabbed from the floor was a pile of soft, gray fur. Cat fur, if I had to guess.

"Rae," Valen said from the other room.

I jerked my head up. He only called me by my real name when something bad happened.

The mercenary walked from the archway that Fraya had claimed led to the kitchen. He held a painting in one hand and offered it to me. I gripped it softly, turning it toward the moonlight to see better.

A group of professors clustered before the entrance to the College of Magic and Mages. The artist had captured their likeliness well, and I recognized Magnolia at the very center, a lopsided smile on her lips. None of the professors in the image even slightly resembled Fraya.

"Where did you find this?" I asked.

"On the wall in the kitchen."

The kitchen. I hadn't seen the kitchen during my visit.

"This isn't a house Fraya was renting," I said.

Valen shook his head. "This was Magnolia's house. And Fraya took it."

I rubbed the downy fur between my fingers. "I think she took more from Magnolia than her house."

<h1 style="text-align:center">Chapter 24</h1>

The Sheriff's Station was the last place I wanted to go to. Even though I missed Krissa, I didn't want to see her again until we had the evidence we needed to set her free. And we didn't have anything. Without a comparison expert, the magic cast was useless. Castor refused to give us the letter from Krissa's house, which may contain a specific scent or fingerprints. Even knowing Fraya was likely involved in Magnolia's murder, and stole the Nightingale, didn't get us any closer to actually finding her.

But suspecting the feather left by Fraya's bird matched that of Magnolia's Nightingale cat wasn't enough. We needed specific proof, which meant Leof needed to compare the scent of the feather-turned-fur to that of the fur found on the body.

I froze when Valen and I stepped into the first hallway. Castor and another man stood on each side of the hall, chatting easily with each other.

Castor glanced at us, a sneer crossing his face. He gave an almost smile, the kind where he showed teeth, but his lips didn't really curve up at all.

The man across from him was tall, really tall, and fairly slim. He wore a deep brown uniform with a sparkling golden badge bearing the seal of Erline on his chest. The Sheriff had arrived—half a day early.

He smiled at me. "You must be the new Crime Investigation Expert I've heard so much about."

He held out his hand, pausing for a moment at the sight of Bubbles nestled in my arms. I returned the greeting without explaining the warplog. "Sir," I stammered. How was I supposed to interact with this man? *Hello, I'm planning to kill you if you put my best friend on an unfair trial.*

"Please, call me Jean. Everyone else does." Sheriff Jean winked at me, then looked to Valen. His gaze narrowed. "Valen," he said flatly.

"Jean," Valen replied, equally neutral.

I looked between the two. They clearly knew each other, but neither offered any additional information.

"Unfortunately, I've got to be off. There's a trial in the morning and I'll need to go over the materials to be prepared." Jean tipped his head. "Evening."

Once the sheriff disappeared, I rounded on Castor and shoved a finger into his face. The constable froze with a wide-eyed expression of shock.

"I swear, if you put Krissa to trial when you know she didn't commit any crime, I will see your guts on the outside of your body. I will skin you alive with a smile on my face and make sure no one ever finds your body. I will walk on the shards of your bones and laugh every time one of them crunch beneath my feet, you son of a—"

Valen grabbed my shoulders and pulled me away. "He gets the point, Sunshine. We're here to prevent that from happening, remember? Let's leave the trash in the hallway and go talk to the marshal now."

Valen pulled me toward Leof's office, but I sent Castor a glare over my shoulder and a pulse of power, so he remembered that I was dangerous too.

I pulled free from Valen's grip and angrily stormed into Leof's office. I slammed down the jar containing the fur sample from Magnolia's house. Bubbles gave a little surprised jump in my arm.

"I need a scent map."

He blinked at me. "You found the Nightingale?"

"I won't know that until you do a scent map."

Valen grabbed my shoulders again. "What's with you tonight? Not that the angry determination isn't attractive, but it's not like you, Sunshine. Here, sit down." He plopped me into one of the twin armchairs before the fire and threw a light blanket over my lap. He tugged the warplog from my grip, making Bubbles groan in protest, but settled him across my legs instead. Bubbles put his head on my leg and licked his eyes with contentment.

I didn't want to sit. I balled my hands into fists. Anger and frustration made my body shake and my mind spin. Krissa needed to get free. Maybe I shouldn't wait for the trail. Maybe I could break her out of prison tonight . . .

"Take this." Valen pressed a mug into my hand. The rich smell of a simple green tea seeped from the cup.

I eyed it wearily. "Last time you gave me tea, it was drugged."

Leof sputtered.

"Unfortunately, I've left my sedative tea at home. You'll have to make do with the regular stuff. Now sip your tea and relax before you scare the wolf too much to do his work."

"She's not scaring me," Leof growled, but he didn't protest Valen's orders.

An unbeckoned exhaustion flowed over me. I leaned my head against the back of the chair. I'd hardly had any sleep over the last few days. Constantly worrying about Krissa and fighting the Shadow-Beasts with Suzie, everything demanded more and more of me.

I was tired.

But I didn't have time to sleep. We were so close to having everything we needed to clear Krissa's name. The sheriff was preparing for a trial. A clock ticked back and forth in my mind, each strike coming closer to forcing my hand to assure Krissa's freedom.

Valen and Leof talked quietly. The fire popped and crackled.

I closed my eyes.

Some part of me recognized when someone sat in the chair beside me.

"You have to take care of yourself if you want to take care of anyone else," a voice said, from my dreams, perhaps. "You are important."

A gentle sleep carried me away.

* * *

I jolted upright. Bubbles yelped as he flopped onto the ground, his legs pawing the air. The blanket slipped from my lap and pooled over top of the warplog. The mug I'd fallen asleep holding had been placed on the short table nestled between the two chairs. Someone must have set it there before it spilled in my slumber.

Leof froze, half bent over the chair. One hand extended

where it had touched my shoulder moments ago and startled me awake.

"I've finished the scent map and comparison of the fur found on Magnolia's body and the transforming feather you found at the house." He paused, probably waiting for the confusion to fade from my sleepy eyes. "They're a match. Magnolia's cat and Fraya's bird are the same creature—the Nightingale."

I blinked while his words soaked into my mind. Bubbles peeked his head from beneath the blanket. He studied the room with large eyes, then burrowed back into the fabric, likely going back to sleep.

"Fraya must have killed Magnolia," I said slowly, trying to make all the pieces fit. "She wanted the Nightingale for herself. Once Krissa found the body, Fraya had the perfect person to frame for the crime."

Leof nodded. "She pretended to be a magic cast expert to get closer to the investigation."

"And I walked her into the morgue." I pressed my palms against my eyes. "She took the Nightingale into the morgue. Once Suzie passed out, Fraya had plenty of time without witnesses to turn Magnolia's body to ash."

"Suzie *passed out*?" Surprise stained Leof's voice.

"Everyone passes out their first time in the morgue," I said absently. "So, we know Fraya killed Magnolia to steal the Nightingale. She framed Krissa for the crime and became involved in the investigation to eliminate additional evidence. But I don't understand why she's still in Hallow's Promise. Fraya has one of the most powerful creatures in existence and she's basically flaunting it around town."

"Her alibi isn't complete yet," Valen said from where he leaned against Leof's desk. "She needs to make sure that Krissa is convicted of the crime to assure nobody looks into the case again."

"But with the scent maps matching, we should have enough information to at least delay the trial. The sheriff may order Castor to give you the letter from Krissa's house to search for additional evidence." Leof stalked around the room, a wolfy, amber color glistening in his eyes. "I think we can actually clear Krissa's name without ever going to trial."

The river of fear in my gut slowed. I trusted Leof. If he felt we were close to setting Krissa free, I believed him wholeheartedly.

"We need to find Fraya and the Nightingale before they finally leave Hallow's Promise," I said.

An angry roar rose from the core of the earth itself. The ground shook, the flames in the fire stretched upward into the chimney, growing hot enough to send sweat instantly across my face. I snatched Bubbles, blanket and all, and retreated as far from the fire as possible.

The shaking stopped, replaced by an eerie stillness in its wake.

Valen looked at me. Ice poured from his body, the kind that fire and heat could never melt. His anger mixed with mine, awakening my magic, sending a hot rage through me.

"I think we've found her," he said. "She's here."

"Why would she be here?" Leof snapped, but another groan escaped from the ground, eliminating any doubts.

"Because Krissa might not have a trial after all." Valen's anger turned his words to ice. "What's the next best way to make sure no one ever discovers the truth?"

It took a moment, but I gasped when his words sank in.

"She's here to kill Krissa," I said.

Chapter 25

We raced down the hall. The door leading to the prison cells beneath the Sheriff's Station was shut. Leof clutched the knob but pulled his hand back with a hiss.

Smoke streamed from his palm.

"Stand back," Valen said. His leg flew up, the bottom of his boot impacting the door just above the locking mechanisms. The heavy wooden slab opened with a loud smack. Our rescue attempt would be anything but subtle.

I headed for the stairs, and someone caught my arm.

Leof looked down at me with his brows creased. "You should stay here. It isn't safe for you down there."

My jaw dropped. I wanted to rub my eyes and see if the man disappeared, because surely something so stupid had to be a dream.

"I've fought these beasts before," I snapped, tugging my arm from his grasp. "I've protected your daughter from them. If you think I'm standing here and *watching* you two fight to save my best friend, then you don't know me at all."

I reached over my shoulder and slid the short sword from where it had been resting on my back. After staying behind while Valen searched Magnolia's house, I knew the weapon had to come with me from now on. Leof's eyes widened as he watched me hold the blade at mid guard, my stance and grip perfect.

"Sunshine," Valen called from halfway down the staircase. "I'll need you down here."

I snapped my gaze away from Leof, adjusted Bubbles in my left arm with the blade in my right. When I passed the section of the door Valen had kicked down, ice crystals clung to the wood. One day, I'd find out exactly what and who the mercenary was.

Shadows clung to every part of the prison cells. The torches hung unlit in their brackets, but the shadows weren't from simple darkness. No, they were a fog, a mist, climbing their way from the split in the ground at the far end of the hallway. They had teeth and claws and scratched at us, unable to leave a mark but emitting a high-pitched laughter, anyway.

The ground had cleaved in two with ugly, jagged lines. At the very end of one split stood the Nightingale. The bird's eyes were clouded and pinched, either with exhaustion or pain. Its long talons dug into the ground and heavy, powerful magic made it hard to breathe.

It was impressive—and terrifying. My faith in our victory dwindled slightly.

Low growls echoed from the walls. Two Shadow-Beasts stalked from the mist. Their green eyes glowed with unnatural light. They bared their teeth, saliva hitting the ground.

"I'll try to stop the Nightingale from calling any more Shadow-Beasts. You go help Krissa." Valen spun his sword in a tight circle, a half-smile on his face. "Yell if you need me."

"She won't need you," Leof said, at my side. "I'll go with her."

The mercenary gave him a cold look, but nodded once. Then he was gone.

Krissa's cell door was open and two dark figures stood inside.

Fraya was taller than Krissa by several inches. She wore a long, blue robe edged in silver that flicked among the shadows with a life of its own. Her fingers wrapped around Krissa's neck, pulling my friend to the tips of her toes.

I lunged for the cell, halting when a Shadow-Beast darted in my path. I rolled, barely missing its frantic snap.

We circled each other. Krissa wouldn't survive long enough for me to fight the creature.

Another canine shape impacted the beast. I yelped as Leof, in his werewolf form, grabbed the creature by the back of the neck and gave it a hard shake. He hadn't bothered to shed his clothing before changing shape, and his tunic and breeches hung awkwardly from his wolf body. Slices of the magical bread I'd given him spilled from his pockets and littered the ground, cascading across the hallway and into the cells.

The Shadow-Beast tore away from Leof's grasp with a growl. Leof glanced at me with amber eyes. His wolf was a brindled brown, out of place amongst the darkness, more at home along the trunks of thick forest trees. He cast a quick glance to Krissa before returning to his opponent.

"Right," I said. "I'll get her."

I hesitated a moment longer, looking for a place to put Bubbles. The cell beside Krissa's was unlocked and empty, so I stuffed him inside and shut the door. He peered from the blanket with a frown across his little face.

"It's just for a minute."

I ran the few steps from Bubbles' cell to Krissa's. My sword cut through the air effortlessly. I heard Tyfin's voice in my head calling out the strike I knew best fit the outcome I wanted.

But Fraya was gone.

Where her hand had wrapped around Krissa's neck, my

sword ran through empty air. I staggered forward and tripped over Krissa where she'd fallen to the ground. I rolled, popping back onto my feet.

I took a moment to study my friend. Her eyes were partially closed, and she gasped for air, but she was alive. It was good enough for now.

A blow hit my upper back between my shoulder blades. The air spilled out of my lungs and pain cascaded down my spine. I staggered, trying to turn, as another strike caught me.

Fraya laughed. "You think yourself a warrior? You come nowhere near my power."

She didn't have a weapon, but the Nightingale must have lent her power somehow. Her limbs moved faster than a blur, streaking toward me with inhumane speed. I flicked my blade up, sending a quick pulse of my magic into it, but was still too slow. Fraya's punch hit the side of my gut, bending me over.

"It didn't have to come to this, you know," she spoke above me. "I planned to give your friend a quick death. It would have looked like suicide. Afterall, murdering one's fellow professors can stir up such grief—I should know."

The pain didn't ease, but my mind took it in and accepted it. Once it had a place of its own, my vision cleared, giving me a line of sight for Fraya's body. I didn't raise my head. I let my breathing sound ragged.

"Now I have this whole mess to clean up. Good thing my pets will assure you're nothing more than dust by the end—"

Her words ended with a scream as I flipped my sword and jabbed it upward into her stomach. A slight hesitation marked the moment the tip found her skin, then it split easily. I pulled the blade back, standing in high guard for my next strike or defense.

She pressed a hand to the wound. Dark red stained her moonlight-colored robe. She lifted her lips. "I liked this outfit."

Fraya backhanded me before I could move the sword again. One moment she sneered, the next, my head spun, a burning flame inside my cheek.

I staggered to the bars of the cell, searching for their support, tripping and falling through the doorway instead. The hard ground caught me. I rolled onto my stomach, tracking each of Fraya's nearing steps. My head swam as I tried to raise the sword toward her approach.

A blur of brown fur and darkness leapt over the top of me. Leof growled as the Shadow-Beast wrestled him onto the ground. A chorus of snarls and saliva echoed from the battle. Leof rose again, lunging for the beast.

A second creature appeared from the side. It plowed into Leof's gut, smacking the werewolf against the opposite wall of the hallway.

"Leof!" I yelled. The sound made my head spin again.

The werewolf didn't get up.

"Leof," the word became a sob.

Distantly, almost lost in shadows, Valen battled more of the beasts at the end of the prison, slowly gaining ground toward the Nightingale.

It wouldn't be enough.

I forced myself onto my side. It didn't really hurt anymore. My body felt heavy, and my head was cloudy. My arms whined and shook as I struggled to rise. But I did it. I stood on trembling knees, blinking wildly to try to clear my vision, and held the sword out.

I was not helpless. I would not die laying down.

"Don't you know when to give up?" Fraya asked, laughing,

laughing at me.

Never, I wanted to say, but the air seemed too thin for words. Or my lungs ached too much.

She pulled in more power from the Nightingale. I tensed, trying to track her movement, but preparing for impact.

Another shadow jumped onto Fraya's back with a ragged scream.

"Nobody hurts my best friend!" Krissa cried.

She wrapped her arms around Fraya's neck and locked her ankles around the woman's waist. Fraya thrashed and tried to reach behind to pluck Krissa from her back. Krissa tightened her hold and dropped one hand to fumble for something in her pocket.

If Krissa distracted Fraya long enough, I could get in the right strike to end it.

I stepped forward. Dizziness twisted my stomach as a sharp pain cut up from my side. I crouched on the ground and threw up on the stones.

I coughed and wiped my mouth, trying to stand again, trying to see the two women.

Fraya staggered around, attempting to bang Krissa into the walls to peel her away. Krissa didn't budge. She'd managed to wrestle out what she'd been grabbing in her pocket: a slice of the magic bread from Leof's pants.

"I don't know what this is," Krissa said. She grabbed Fraya's hair and pulled her head back harshly. "But if Rae made it, it's going to do something."

She stuffed the food into Fraya's mouth.

The woman tried to spit it out, but the magic burned in my chest as she swallowed some of it. Krissa dropped from her back, breathing hard.

Fraya clutched her throat. She looked at me, cinnamon crumbs falling from her lips, my death in her eyes.

She made it one step, then collapsed to her knees.

The power fell away from her. The shadows stopped laughing at us. One by one, they slid away, back into whatever dimension the Nightingale called them from. Sparks of light erupted as the torches lit one by one. The remaining Shadow-Beasts dissolved.

But the bread didn't stop there.

Fraya reached her hands out, studying them. "What have you done?" she hissed. The dark coloring of her hair faded into a lighter blonde. Her face changed slightly, just enough to widen the narrow cheekbones and elongate her nose. The bread had stripped away whatever concealment spell she'd been using since murdering Magnolia—revealing who she truly was.

"Irabel?" Krissa rose to her knees. "Irabel, *you* murdered Magnolia."

But Professor Irabel Ironhand didn't glance at Krissa. She looked at *me*.

"*You*. You will die."

She lunged, a knife appearing from somewhere. I tried to move, to navigate a simple dodging technique, but shards of glass tried to slice me from the inside out. I'd broken at least one rib, probably more.

"I don't think so, bitch." Krissa jumped on top of the woman again. Irabel's blade fell from her hand and Krissa snatched it. She plunged the knife through Irabel's shoulder, trapping her against the stone floor.

Irabel screamed, followed by a plethora of curses.

"You were a terrible professor and an even worse murderer," Krissa said. "Now shut up."

Krissa staggered to me and collapsed on the ground. Valen was checking on Leof, so I sagged beside my friend. We ignored Irabel's curses as she tried to pry the blade, trapping her to the ground.

"You came," Krissa said.

"Of course I did." Every word was agony, but I said them anyway. "I'll always be there, Krissa."

She smiled. "Thanks."

Valen leaned over us. His dark eyes danced with humor. "The werewolf will be alright. I'll just have to treat him with some of that healing balm for the bite wounds. But I may wait until they start smoking."

"Valen." I let disappointment leak into the word.

He winked. "Only kidding, Sunshine." Scratching sounds came from the far area of the prison hall. "I think someone else is here to see you."

The Nightingale walked slowly toward us. Its head bent low, its beak parted as it breathed heavily. He whined when he got to us and nuzzled Krissa's hand. The gray feathers stripped away, creating a pile on the ground, and revealing a round-ish creature with careful spines along its back.

"A hoglet," Krissa said. She stroked its spines and the Nightingale hoglet laid down against her side. He closed his eyes, sleep overcoming it.

"It's chosen you as its new owner," Valen said. "It is a great honor."

Krissa circled her hand around the creature. "I'll call it Whiskers, like Magnolia wanted."

I laid my head on the hard ground beside Krissa and Whiskers. At some point, Valen let Bubbles out of his cell and he hopped onto my stomach with a grunt.

I never wanted to move again.

Chapter 26

Valen, Suzie, Leof, Krissa, Bubbles, and Whiskers all sat in my house and watched me make tea. We wore cuts, bruises, bite marks, and pure exhaustion. But nobody wanted to leave yet. Maybe it felt safer when we were all together.

The cauldron boiled from its place on the fire. I ground a deep black tea into a fine powder in the mortar and portioned a generous amount into each cup. I swirled a dose of honey, lavender syrup, and spiced rum into each. The water spilled on top, only enough to cover the concoction. It had to set for a minute.

My wards pulsed before someone knocked on the door.

Valen stood and opened the door. He talked to whoever was on the other side for a moment, then pushed the door wide open so we could all see.

Castor stood on my stoop, his lips pressed tight in shame.

"He says he's here to apologize," Valen said.

"I *am* here to apologize. I was hasty in my accusation, and it almost got a lot of people hurt." Or killed. "And for that, I am deeply sorry."

I gave Castor my biggest smile. I tried to hide all the anger. I wanted my eyes to look clear, innocent. "It's okay, Castor. We understand you had a job to do. Why don't you come inside and join us for tea?"

His jaw fell. "I—uh—that's not necessary."

I curled my fingers and flicked them in a *come here* motion. "Please, I insist."

He hesitated. I thought he would refuse, but he ducked his head sort of sheepishly and stepped over my threshold.

My wards yelled in my mind and a pulse of power ran through the house.

Castor's eyes widened. A pathetic squeak emitted from his mouth before both hands clutched at his crotch. He fell to his knees, eyes rolling into the back of his head.

I walked to the front door, slowly, enjoying each second of agony the man felt as my Lighting-Crotch spell attacked him.

"If you ever step foot on my property again, I'll have a Fire-Crotch spell ready, and you really don't want to see what's left after that one." I slammed the door, savoring the small cries that came through the wood.

"Fire-Crotch?" Krissa asked. "Does that exist?"

I shrugged. "Probably."

I filtered the tea leaves from the syrup and added the rest of the water. Everyone grabbed a mug, found a seat, and a collective sigh of relief escaped through the room.

***

***

Wonder what Valen's up to next? Subscribe to my newsletter and read the free BONUS chapter to find out more! Visit https://subscribepage.io/gHkKZv or scan the QR code below:

Want to Support the Author?

The easiest way is to leave a review on your favorite reading platform. Reviews help us get visibility in the community, and spread our books to a wider audience.

Whether or not you choose to leave a review, THANK YOU for being here and reading our books.

Acknowledgements

Another thank you to my editor, Nicole at The Assist, LLC. Thank you for pouring yourself into this book despite the turbulence of life.

Thank you to GetCovers for creating the cover and dealing with multiple revisions to get just the right color blue.

As always, thank you to my family. My husband for wrestling the kids so I could get this book finished. And to my children for keeping me on my toes, even if I do wish you'd sleep as much as Bubbles does.

And finally, THANK YOU to all my readers. It is an honor that you choose to spend your time with me and my worlds. One *thank you* can never be enough <3

About the Author

A.N. Payton is a fantasy romance author, true-crime obsessee, and a very low-skilled seamstress. She writes at the intersection of fantasy and science, with a dash (or overflowing scoop) of romance. Her books are concocted with the perfect proportions of strong female characters, sexy men who may or may not end up shirtless, and plenty of sarcastic banter.

A.N. Payton spends her days at a top-secret job (if she told you, she'd have to kill you), which proves real life is more wild than fiction. At night she escapes by writing new worlds and problems for someone else to solve - probably with a sword.

She lives in the pacific northwest with a husband she loves (depending on the day), two kids she loves (most of the time), and a dog she loves (all the time).

Other Works by A.N. Payton

Princess Sal's magic bought her people peace and security, but she'll never be safe with the vampire king in her castle.

Centuries of war come to a bitter end when Princess Sal's parents steal half the witch army and disappear. Sal is forced to surrender to the vampire king, Kadence, and bind her magic as part of their agreement. She will give anything to protect her people – anything except her heart.

When Kadence conquers the witch kingdom, he doesn't expect their princess to be as delicious as wild honey. He can't decide if he'd rather kiss or kill Sal, and his desire for her battles against his hatred of witches. Despite their attraction, Kadence can't forget their war-torn history. He must decide if he can overcome his past to make way for a new future – one that might include Sal.

But when scouts locate Sal's parents and discover they're

marching a demon army toward the kingdom, Sal and Kadence must unite their people for a final battle. If they don't, bloodthirsty demons will consume everyone they vowed to protect. Can they work together to save their people, or will hellfire destroy them all?